SHUSA

D0447965

FIVE
BY
ENDO

STORIES

Translated by Van C. Gessel

A NEW DIRECTIONS

Manufactured in the United States of America
New Directions Books are printed on acid-free paper.

First published as a New Directions Bibelot in 2000
Published simultaneously in Canada by Penguin Books Canada Limited

PUBLISHER'S NOTE : "The Case of Isobe" is the opening chapter of Endo's novel
Deep River in which Mr. Osobe is one of a group of Japanese travelers on tour in
India. Although this excerpt does not bring his story to conclusion, the Publisher
feels it stands well alone.

Library of Congress Cataloging-in-Publication Data

Endo, Shusaku, 1923-1996
    Five by Endo: stories / Shusaku Endo; translated by Van C. Gessel
            p. cm.
    Contents: Unzen—A fifty-year-old-man—Japanese in Warsaw—The box—The
case of Isobe.
    ISBN 0-8112-1439-7 (pb : alk.)
    1. Endå, Shåsaku, 1923-1996 - Translations into English. I. Gessel, Van C. II. Title.
PL849.N4 A23 2000
895.6'35—dc21   99-056269

New Directions Books are published for James Laughlin
by New Directions Publishing Corporation
80 Eighth Avenue, New York 10011

Contents

FIVE BY ENDO

UNZEN

As he sat on the bus for Unzen, he drank a bottle of milk and gazed blankly at the rain-swept sea. The frosty waves washed languidly against the shore just beneath the coastal highway.

The bus had not yet left the station. The scheduled hour of departure had long since passed, but a connecting bus from Nagasaki still had not arrived, and their driver was chatting idly with the woman conductor and displaying no inclination to switch on the engine. Even so the tolerant passengers uttered no word of complaint, but merely pressed their faces against the window glass. A group of bathers from the hot springs walked by, dressed in large, thickly-padded kimonos. They shielded themselves from the rain with umbrellas borrowed from their inn. The counters of the gift shops were lined with all sorts of decorative shells and souvenir bean-jellies from the local hot springs, but there were no customers around to buy their wares.

'This place reminds me of Atagawa in Izu,' Suguro grumbled to himself as he snapped the cardboard top back onto the milk bottle. 'What a disgusting landscape.'

He had to chuckle a bit at himself for coming all the way to this humdrum spot at the western edge of Kyushu. In Tokyo he had not had the slightest notion that this village of Obama, home of many of the Christian martyrs and some of the participants in the Shimabara Rebellion, would be so commonplace a town.

From his studies of the Christian era in Japan, Suguro knew that around 1630 many of the faithful had made the climb from Obama towards Unzen, which a Jesuit of the day had called 'one of the tallest mountains in Japan'. The Valley of Hell high up on Unzen was an ideal place for torturing Christians. According to the records, after 1629, when the Nagasaki Magistrate Takenaka Shigetsugu hit upon the idea of abusing the Christians in this hot spring inferno, sixty or seventy prisoners a day were roped together and herded from Obama to the top of this mountain.

Now tourists strolled the streets of the village, and popular songs

1

blared out from loudspeakers. Nothing remained to remind one of that sanguinary history. But precisely three centuries before the present month of January, on a day of misty rain, the man whose footsteps Suguro now hoped to retrace had undoubtedly climbed up this mountain from Obama.

Finally the engine started up, and the bus made its way through the village. They passed through a district of two- and three-storey Japanese inns, where men leaned with both hands on the railings of the balconies and peered down into the bus. Even those windows which were deserted were draped with pink and white washcloths and towels. When the bus finally passed beyond the hotel district, both sides of the mountain road were lined with old stone walls and squat farmhouses with thatched roofs.

Suguro had no way of knowing whether these walls and farmhouses had existed in the Christian century. Nor could he be sure that this road was the one travelled by the Christians, the officers, and the man he was pursuing. The only certain thing was that, during their fitful stops along the path, they had looked up at this same Mount Unzen wrapped in grey mist.

He had brought a number of books with him from Tokyo, but he now regretted not including a collection of letters from Jesuits of the day who had reported on the Unzen martyrdoms to their superiors in Rome. He had thoughtlessly tossed into his bag one book that would be of no use to him on this journey – Collado's *Christian Confessions*.

The air cooled as the bus climbed into the hills, and the passengers, peeling skins from the mikans they had bought at Obama, listened half-heartedly to the sing-song travelogue provided by the conductor.

'Please look over this way,' she said with a waxy smile. 'There are two large pine trees on top of the hill we are about to circle. It's said that at about this spot, the Christians of olden days would turn around and look longingly back at the village of Obama. These trees later became known as the Looking-Back Pines.'

Collado's *Christian Confessions* was published in Rome in 1632, just five years before the outbreak of the Shimabara Rebellion. By that time the shogunate's persecution of the Christians had grown fierce, but a few Portuguese and Italian missionaries had still managed to steal into Japan from Macao or Manila. The *Christian Confessions* were printed as a practical guide to Japanese grammar for the benefit of these missionaries. But what Suguro found hard to understand was why Collado had made public the confessions of these Japanese Christians, when a

Catholic priest was under no circumstances permitted to reveal the innermost secrets of the soul shared with him by members of his flock.

Yet the night he read the *Confessions*, Suguro felt as though a more responsive chord had been struck within him than with any other history of the Christian era he had encountered. Every study he had read was little more than a string of paeans to the noble acts of priests and martyrs and common believers inspired by faith. They were without exception chronicles of those who had sustained their beliefs and their testimonies no matter what sufferings or tortures they had to endure. And each time he read them, Suguro had to sigh, 'There's no way I can emulate people like this.'

He had been baptized as a child, along with the rest of his family. Since then he had passed through many vicissitudes and somehow managed to arrive in his forties without rejecting his religion. But that was not due to firm resolve or unshakeable faith. He was more than adequately aware of his own spiritual slovenliness and pusillanimity. He was certain that an unspannable gulf separated him from the ancient martyrs of Nagasaki, Edo and Unzen who had effected glorious martyrdoms. Why had they all been so indomitable?

Suguro diligently searched the Christian histories for someone like himself. But there was no one to be found. Finally he had stumbled across the *Christian Confessions* one day in a second-hand bookshop, and as he flipped indifferently through the pages of the book, he had been moved by the account of a man whose name Collado had concealed. The man had the same feeble will and tattered integrity as Suguro. Gradually he had formed in his mind an image of this man – genuflecting like a camel before the priest nearly three hundred years earlier, relishing the almost desperate experience of exposing his own filthiness to the eyes of another.

'I stayed for a long time with some heathens. I didn't want the innkeeper to realize I was a Christian, so I went with him often to the heathen temples and chanted along with them. Many times when they praised the gods and buddhas, I sinned greatly by nodding and agreeing with them. I don't remember how many times I did that. Maybe twenty or thirty times – more than twenty, anyway.

'And when the heathens and the apostates got together to slander us Christians and blaspheme against God, I was there with them. I didn't try to stop them talking or to refute them.

'Just recently, at the Shōgun's orders the Magistrate came to our fief from the capital, determined to make all the Christians here apostatize.

Everyone was interrogated and pressed to reject the Christian codes, or at least to apostatize in form only. Finally, in order to save the lives of my wife and children, I told them I would abandon my beliefs.'

Suguro did not know where this man had been born, or what he had looked like. He had the impression he was a samurai, but there was no way to determine who his master might have been. The man would have had no inkling that his private confession would one day be published in a foreign land, and eventually fall into the hands of one of his own countrymen again, to be read by a person like Suguro. Though he did not have a clear picture of how the man looked, Suguro had some idea of the assortment of facial expressions he would have had to employ in order to evade detection. If he had been born in that age, Suguro would have had no qualms about going along with the Buddhist laymen to worship at their temples, if that meant he would not be exposed as a Christian. When someone mocked the Christian faith, he would have lowered his eyes and tried to look unconcerned. If so ordered, he might even have written out an oath of apostasy, if that would mean saving the lives of his family as well as his own.

A faint ray of light tentatively penetrated the clouds that had gathered over the summit of Unzen. Maybe it will clear up, he thought. In summer this paved road would no doubt be choked by a stream of cars out for a drive, but now there was only the bus struggling up the mountain with intermittent groans. Groves of withered trees shivered all around. A cluster of rain-soaked bungalows huddled silently among the trees, their doors tightly shut.

'Listen, martyrdom is no more than a matter of pride.'

He had had this conversation in the corner of a bar in Shinjuku. A pot of Akita salted-fish broth simmered in the centre of the *sake*-stained table. Seated around the pot, Suguro's elders in the literary establishment had been discussing the hero of a novel he had recently published. The work dealt with some Christian martyrs in the 1870s. The writers at the gathering claimed that they could not swallow the motivations behind those martyrdoms the way Suguro had.

'At the very core of this desire to be a martyr you'll find pride, pure and simple.'

'I'm sure pride plays a part in it. Along with the desire to become a hero, and even a touch of insanity, perhaps. But –'

Suguro fell silent and clutched his glass. It was a simple task to pinpoint elements of heroism and pride among the motives for martyr-dom. But when those elements were obliterated residual motives still remained. Those residual motives were of vital importance.

'Well, if you're going to look at it that way, you can find pride and selfishness underlying virtually every human endeavour, every single act of good faith.'

In the ten years he had been writing fiction, Suguro had grown increasingly impatient with those modern novelists who tried to single out the egotism and pride in every act of man. To Suguro's mind, such a view of humanity entailed the loss of something of consummate value, like water poured through a sieve.

The road wound its way to the summit through dead grass and barren woods. In days past, lines of human beings had struggled up this path. Both pride and madness had certainly been part of their make-up, but there must have been something more to it.

'The right wing during the war, for instance, had a certain martyr mentality. I can't help thinking there's something impure going on when people are intoxicated by something like that. But perhaps I feel that way because I experienced the war myself,' one of his elders snorted as he drank down his cup of tepid *sake*. Sensing an irreconcilable mis-understanding between himself and this man, Suguro could only grin acquiescently.

Before long he caught sight of a column of white smoke rising like steam from the belly of the mountain. Though the windows of the bus were closed, he smelled a faintly sulphuric odour. Milky white crags and sand came into clear focus.

'Is that the Valley of Hell?'

'No.' The conductor shook her head. 'It's a little further up.'

A tiny crack in the clouds afforded a glimpse of blue sky. The bus, which up until now had panted along, grinding its gears, suddenly seemed to catch its breath and picked up speed. The road had levelled off, then begun to drop. A series of arrows tacked to the leafless trees, apparently to guide hikers, read 'Valley of Hell'. Just ahead was the red roof of the rest-house.

Suguro did not know whether the man mentioned in the *Confessions* had come here to the Valley of Hell. But, as if before Suguro's eyes, the image of another individual had overlapped with that of the first man and now stumbled along with his head bowed. There was a little more detailed information about this second man. His name was Kichijirō, and he first appeared in the historical records on the fifth day of

December, 1631, when seven priests and Christians were tortured at the Valley of Hell. Kichijirō came here to witness the fate of the fathers who had cared for him. He had apostatized much earlier, so he had been able to blend in with the crowd of spectators. Standing on tiptoe, he had witnessed the cruel punishments which the officers inflicted on his spiritual mentors.

Father Christovao Ferreira, who later broke under torture and left a filthy smudge on the pages of Japanese Christian history, sent to his homeland a letter vividly describing the events of that day. The seven Christians arrived at Obama on the evening of December the second, and were driven up the mountain all the following day. There were several look-out huts on the slope, and that evening the seven captives were forced into one of them, their feet and hands still shackled. There they awaited the coming of dawn.

'The tortures commenced on the fifth of December in the following manner. One by one each of the seven was taken to the brink of the seething pond. There they were shown the frothy spray from the boiling water, and ordered to renounce their faith. The air was chilly and the hot water of the pond churned so furiously that, had God not sustained them, a single look would have cause them to faint away. They all shouted, "Torture us! We will not recant!" At this response, the guards stripped the garments from the prisoners' bodies and bound their hands and feet. Four of them held down a single captive as a ladle holding about a quarter of a litre was filled with the boiling water. Three ladlesful were slowly poured over each body. One of the seven, a young girl called Maria, fainted from the excruciating pain and fell to the ground. In the space of thirty-three days, each of them was subjected to this torture a total of six times.'

Suguro was the last one off when the bus came to a stop. The cold, taut mountain air blew a putrid odour into his nostrils. White steam poured onto the highway from the tree-ringed valley.

'How about a photograph? Photographs, anyone?' a young man standing beside a large camera on a tripod called out to Suguro. 'I'll pay the postage wherever you want to send it.'

At various spots along the road stood women proffering eggs in baskets and waving clumsily-lettered signs that read 'Boiled Eggs'. They too touted loudly for business.

Weaving their way among these hawkers, Suguro and the rest of the group from the bus walked towards the valley. The earth, overgrown with shrubbery, was virtually white, almost the colour of flesh stripped clean of its layer of skin. The rotten-smelling steam gushed ceaselessly from amid the trees. The narrow path stitched its way back and forth between springs of hot, bubbling water. Some parts of the white-speckled pools lay as calm and flat as a wall of plaster; others eerily spewed up slender sprays of gurgling water. Here and there on the hillocks formed from sulphur flows. stood pine trees scorched red by the heat.

The bus passengers extracted boiled eggs from their paper sacks and stuffed them into their mouths. They moved forward like a column of ants.

'Come and look over here. There's a dead bird.'

'So there is. I suppose the gas fumes must have asphyxiated it.'

All he knew for certain was that Kichijirō had been a witness to those tortures. Why had he come? There was no way of knowing whether he had joined the crowd of Buddhist spectators in the hope of rescuing the priests and the faithful who were being tormented. The only tangible piece of information he had about Kichijirō was that he had forsworn his religion to the officers, 'so that his wife and children might live'. Nevertheless, he had followed in the footsteps of those seven Christians, walking all the way from Nagasaki to Obama, then trudging to the top of the bitterly cold peak of Unzen.

Suguro could almost see the look on Kichijirō's face as he stood at the back of the crowd, furtively watching his former companions with the tremulous gaze of a dog, then lowering his eyes in humiliation. That look was very like Suguro's own. In any case, there was no way Suguro could stand in chains before these loathsomely bubbling pools and make any show of courage.

A momentary flash of white lit up the entire landscape; then a fierce eruption burst forth with the smell of noxious gas. A mother standing near the surge quickly picked up her crouching child and retreated. A placard reading 'Dangerous Beyond This Point' was thrust firmly into the clay. Around it the carcasses of three dead swallows were stretched out like mummies.

This must be the spot where the Christians were tortured, he thought. Through a crack in the misty, shifting steam, Suguro saw the black outlines of a cross. Covering his nose and mouth with a handkerchief and balancing precariously near the warning sign, he peered below him. The mottled water churned and sloshed before his eyes. The Christians must have stood just where he was standing now when they were tortured. And Kichijirō would have stayed behind, standing about

7

where the mother and her child now stood at a cautious distance, watching the spectacle with the rest of the crowd. Inwardly, did he ask them to forgive him? Had Suguro been in his shoes, he would have had no recourse but to repeat over and over again, 'Forgive me! I'm not strong enough to be a martyr like you. My heart melts just to think about this dreadful torture.'

Of course, Kichijirō could justify his attitude. If he had lived in a time of religious freedom, he would never have become an apostate. He might not have qualified for sainthood, but he could have been a man who tamely maintained his faith. But to his regret, he had been born in an age of persecution, and out of fear he had tossed away his beliefs. Not everyone can become a saint or a martyr. Yet must those who do not qualify as saints be branded forever with the mark of the traitor? – Perhaps he had made such a plea to the Christians who vilified him. Yet, despite the logic of his argument, he surely suffered pangs of remorse and cursed his own faint resolve.

'The apostate endures a pain none of you can comprehend.'

Over the span of three centuries this cry, like the shriek of a wounded bird, reached Suguro's ears. That single line recorded in the *Christian Confessions* cut at Suguro's chest like a sharp sword. Surely those were the words Kichijirō must have shouted to himself here at Unzen as he looked upon his tormented friends.

They reboarded the bus. The ride from Unzen to Shimabara took less than an hour. A fistful of blue finally appeared in the sky, but the air remained cold. The same conductor forced her usual smile and commented on the surroundings in a sing-song voice.

The seven Christians, refusing to bend to the tortures at Unzen, had been taken down the mountain to Shimabara, along the same route Suguro was now following. He could almost see them dragging their scalded legs, leaning on walking-sticks and enduring lashes from the officers.

Leaving some distance between them, Kichijirō had timorously followed behind. When the weary Christians stopped to catch their breath, Kichijirō also halted, a safe distance behind. He hurriedly crouched down like a rabbit in the overgrowth, lest the officers suspect him, and did not rise again until the group had resumed their trek. He was like a jilted woman plodding along in pursuit of her lover.

Half-way down the mountain he had a glimpse of the dark sea. Milky clouds veiled the horizon; several wan beams of sunlight filtered through the cracks. Suguro thought how blue the ocean would appear on a clear day.

'Look – you can see a blur out there that looks like an island. Unfortunately, you can't see it very well today. This is Dangō Island, where Amakusa Shirō, the commander of the Christian forces, planned the Shimabara Rebellion with his men.'

At this the passengers took a brief, apathetic glance towards the island. Before long the view of the distant sea was blocked by a forest of trees.

What must those seven Christians have felt as they looked at this ocean? They knew they would soon be executed at Shimabara. The corpses of martyrs were swiftly reduced to ashes and cast upon the seas. If that were not done, the remaining Christians would surreptitiously worship the clothing and even locks of hair from the martyrs as though they were holy objects. And so the seven, getting their first distant view of the ocean from this spot, must have realized that it would be their grave. Kichijirō too would have looked at the sea, but with a different kind of sorrow – with the knowledge that the strong ones in the world of faith were crowned with glory, while the cowards had to carry their burdens with them throughout their lives.

When the group reached Shimabara, four of them were placed in a cell barely three feet tall and only wide enough to accommodate one tatami. The other three were jammed into another room equally cramped. As they awaited their punishment, they persistently encouraged one another and went on praying. There is no record of where Kichijirō stayed during this time.

The village of Shimabara was dark and silent. The bus came to a stop by a tiny wharf where the rickety ferry-boat to Amakusa was moored forlornly. Wood chips and flotsam bobbed on the small waves that lapped at the breakwater. Among the debris floated an object that resembled a rolled-up newspaper; it was the corpse of a cat.

The town extended in a thin band along the seafront. The fences of local factories stretched far into the distance, while the odour of chemicals wafted all the way to the highway.

Suguro set out towards the reconstructed Shimabara Castle. The only signs of life he encountered along the way were a couple of high-school girls riding bicycles.

'Where is the execution ground where the Christians were killed?' he asked them.

'I didn't know there was such a place,' said one of them, blushing. She turned to her friend. 'Have you heard of anything like that? You don't know, do you?' Her friend shook her head.

He came to a neighbourhood identified as a former samurai residence. It had stood behind the castle, where several narrow paths intersected. A crumbling mud wall wound its way between the paths. The drainage ditch was as it had been in those days. Summer mikans poked their heads above the mud wall, which had already blocked out the evening sun. All the buildings were old, dark and musty. They had probably been the residence of a low-ranking samurai, built at the end of the Tokugawa period. Many Christians had been executed at the Shimabara grounds, but Suguro had not come across any historical documents identifying the location of the prison.

He retraced his steps, and after a short walk came out on a street of shops where popular songs were playing. The narrow street was packed with a variety of stores, including gift shops. The water in the drainage ditch was as limpid as water from a spring.

'The execution ground? I know where that is.' The owner of a tobacco shop directed Suguro to a pond just down the road. 'If you go straight on past the pond, you'll come to a nursery school. The execution ground was just to the side of the school.'

Though they say nothing of how he was able to do it, the records indicate that Kichijirō was allowed to visit the seven prisoners on the day before their execution. Possibly he put some money into the hands of the officers.

Kichijirō offered a meagre plate of food to the prisoners, who were prostrate from their ordeal.

'Kichijirō, did you retract your oath?' one of the captives asked compassionately. He was eager to know if the apostate had finally informed the officials that he could not deny his faith. 'Have you come here to see us because you have retracted?'

Kichijirō looked up at them timidly and shook his head.

'In any case, Kichijirō, we can't accept this food.'

'Why not?'

'Why not?' The prisoners were mournfully silent for a moment. 'Because we have already accepted the fact that we will die.'

Kichijirō could only lower his eyes and say nothing. He knew that he himself could never endure the sort of agony he had witnessed at the Valley of Hell on Unzen.

Through his tears he whimpered, 'If I can't suffer the same pain as you, will I be unable to enter Paradise? Will God forsake someone like me?'

He walked along the street of shops as he had been instructed and came to the pond. A floodgate blocked the overflow from the pond, and the water poured underground and into the drainage ditch in the village. Suguro read a sign declaring that the purity of the water in Shimabara village was due to the presence of this pond.

He heard the sounds of children at play. Four or five young children were tossing a ball back and forth in the nursery school playground. The setting sun shone feebly on the swings and sandbox in the yard. He walked around behind a drooping hedge of rose bushes and located the remains of the execution ground, now the only barren patch within a grove of trees.

It was a deserted plot some three hundred square yards in size, grown rank with brown weeds; pines towered over a heap of refuse. Suguro had come all the way from Tokyo to have a look at this place. Or had he made the journey out of a desire to understand better Kichijirō's emotions as he stood in this spot?

The following morning the seven prisoners were hoisted onto the unsaddled horses and dragged through the streets of Shimabara to this execution ground.

One of the witnesses to the scene has recorded the events of the day: 'After they were paraded about, they arrived at the execution ground, which was surrounded by a palisade. They were taken off their horses and made to stand in front of stakes set three metres apart. Firewood was already piled at the base of the stakes, and straw roofs soaked in sea water had been placed on top of them to prevent the flames from raging too quickly and allowing the martyrs to die with little agony. The ropes that bound them to the stakes were tied as loosely as possible, to permit them, up to the very moment of death, to twist their bodies and cry out that they would abandon their faith.

'When the officers began setting fire to the wood, a solitary man broke through the line of guards and dashed towards the stakes. He was shouting something, but I could not hear what he said over the roar of the fires. The fierce flames and smoke prevented the man from approaching the prisoners. The guards swiftly apprehended him and asked if he was a Christian. At that, the man froze in fear, and jabbering, "I am no Christian. I have nothing to do with these people! I just lost my head in all the excitement," he skulked away. But some in the crowd had seen him at the rear of the assemblage, his hands pressed together as he repeated over and over, "Forgive me! Forgive me!"

'The seven victims sang a hymn until the flames enveloped their stakes. Their voices were exuberant, totally out of keeping with the cruel punishment they were even then enduring. When those voices suddenly ceased, the only sound was the dull crackling of wood. The man who had darted forward could be seen walking lifelessly away from the execution ground. Rumours spread through the crowd that he too had been a Christian.'

Suguro noticed a dark patch at the very centre of the execution ground. On closer inspection he discovered several charred stones half buried beneath the black earth. Although he had no way of knowing whether these stones had been used here three hundred years before, when seven Christians had been burned at the stake, he hurriedly snatched up one of the stones and put it in his pocket. Then, his spine bent like Kichijirō's, he walked back towards the road.

A Fifty-year-old Man

'All right , now to the criticisms. Kon-san, when we were doing the waltz, you continued to loosen your grip of your partner.'

'Right.'

'When your grip loosens, you look sloppy. That's what I always say.'

After the group finished dancing, the dance instructor offered criticism to the seven mixed couples as they wiped away their sweat. When this amateur dance group was first formed, renting a classroom at a dressmaking school, a bank employee became their teacher. He was selected because in his college days he had won second place in a nation-wide dance competition.

'Sonny, your rhythm is all off. You still have some bad habits you picked up from cabaret dancing.'

'I understand.'

'Mimi-chan, why is it you turn your face away when you're dancing with Sonny?'

'It's horrible. He had some pot-stickers to eat today before he came here.'

While the others laughed the instructor grinned feebly, and finally he looked towards Chiba and simply remarked: 'Mr Chiba, you still look at your feet from time to time. You need to have more confidence in your steps.'

The teacher called the others in the group by pet names like Kon-san, Mimi-chan or Sonny, but Chiba alone he referred to deferentially as 'Mr Chiba'. Chiba was past fifty, considerably older than anyone else in the dance group.

'That's all for today.'

Everyone pitched in to return the desks and chairs that had been pushed to a corner of the room to their original position, after which they went out into the deserted, dusty-smelling hallway. An inconsequential drizzle was falling outside, but the moisture felt good on their sweat-soaked foreheads. When they reached the road leading to the railway station, the young people turned to head for a bar, but Chiba alone bid them farewell. The young people all bowed to him. He hailed an unoccupied taxi, and when he sank down into the back seat, forgetting even that there was a driver, he muttered to himself: 'Ah, I'm so tired!' It was hard work at his age to dance for an hour and a half without a break, and again today he was stiff from his thighs down to his ankles.

'Is something wrong?' the driver, looking back, asked with concern.

'It's nothing,' Chiba answered vaguely. He was embarrassed to be out dancing at his age. Even his wife gave him a strange look when he announced that he was going to learn to dance in order to tone up his legs, which had become quite frail. Why not golf? she inquired. I don't like golf, it takes up too much time. I wanted to learn how to dance when I was young, but I couldn't because of the war. Just an old man's stubbornness? What are you talking about? I'm not all that old yet. He bluntly brushed aside his wife's suggestion.

'How's business?'

'Not good at all.' The driver shrugged his shoulders. 'Last year, I didn't even have to go out looking for customers, they'd come looking for me. But now all of us drivers are falling over each other to snatch away customers. Do you think times'll get better next year? We don't have a union, see. . . .'

A stabbing pain suddenly pierced the back of Chiba's head. It started just at the point where his hair spun in a whorl, and spread in all directions like black ink poured into a glass of water. Chiba clutched at his knees to combat the pain. After all, taxi driving's nothing more than a job to bring in a day's wages.

In a union, anybody who complains just gets the axe. Why, even in my own case . . .

'I'm sorry, but . . .' Chiba panted, 'I've got a terrible headache.'

'Eh? That's awful.' Quickly the driver proposed: 'Would you like to go to a hospital?'

'No, I'll be fine. It'll go away soon.'

This was not the first time he'd experienced such a headache. They had afflicted him without warning three times since last year. He knew the cause. When he went without sleep or engaged in activities too strenuous for a man his age, his blood pressure would suddenly climb as high as 200. At such times, Chiba was invariably stricken with a migraine.

'Are you sure you're all right?' The driver seemed less concerned than anxious that something tiresome might happen in his taxi. 'Don't you think you ought to go to a hospital?'

'I'm all right.'

When he closed his eyes and controlled his breathing, the intense pain gradually subsided, like a toothache yielding to an analgesic. Afterwards a dull ache that he was able to endure lingered on for about a day. As he leaned his body against the window of the vehicle, it occurred to him that his mother had died of a stroke when she was fifty-four. The first time he'd had his blood pressure taken, the doctor had asked him if any of his relatives had suffered a stroke. And he had been informed many times that this condition was inherited.

'Well, then,' Chiba jested as he always did, 'I won't have to worry about dying of cancer, will I? I'd much rather drop dead of a stroke.'

The night his mother died, Chiba had been out partying. He was still burdened with the knowledge that he had been merry-making in his mother's final hour. When the doctor informed him that his blood pressure was high, he actually felt almost happy that he might be able to die in the same manner as his mother.

Once he passed the age of forty-five, Chiba brought the

laughter of his family upon his head by buying up all kinds of folk remedies and dubious pieces of fitness equipment, all in the name of taking care of his health. He gulped down green potions made from bamboo grass and tea brewed from the Chinese matrimony vine; into his bath-tub he inserted a machine that belched up bubbles; and he installed an electric massage chair in the parlour. He tried walking on stalks of green bamboo, and he even bought a cycling machine at an exorbitant price. He stayed with none of them very long, and ultimately his wife had to carry the massage chair and the bicycle out into the shed in the garden. By now he was reduced to taking dancing lessons to strengthen his legs and back, and taking their dog for a walk each day when he had a few free moments.

Chiba had liked dogs since his childhood. He didn't really know why. Perhaps it was because when he was still at elementary school his dog was the only companion to whom he could admit his own grief over the discord and the talk of divorce between his parents.

At that time, his family was living in Dalian in Manchuria. By the end of September in Dalian, nearly half the leaves had fallen from the trees lining the streets, and each day the sky was filled with grey clouds. At school he would perpetually tell jokes and play the clown, but once class was dismissed and he was left on his own, he never wanted to return straight home. He hated to see his gloomy-faced mother, seated in an unlit room like a stone statue. His elder brother, who was in junior high, would come home from school and without a word sit at his desk and open his books. Even as a boy Chiba had been painfully aware that his brother behaved in this manner in an attempt to endure the discord between his parents. When finally he returned home, he did not go in the front door but would hide his school bag in the shade of the fence and roam endlessly outdoors. At such times, his cross-breed dog would follow him wherever he went.

Kicking up the desiccated acacia leaves, he would stare at the Manchurian children playing with their skipping-ropes, or kill time by going to the pond in the park, still not capped with a thick layer of ice, and throw stones at the old boats tethered to piles. The dog would lie down beside him, staring at some vague point in the distance. When the sun began to set, and his kneecaps, exposed below his short trousers, began to ache from the cold evening air, he still didn't want to go home. It hurt him to listen from his room as his father, just home from work, roughly snapped at his mother, and to hear her sobbing voice.

'I just . . . can't take it any more. . . .' Sometimes he would say that to the dog as it gazed into the distance. Since he always played the fool, he couldn't bring himself to confess the anguish he felt to his teachers or his friends at school.

'I can't take it any more.'

The dog looked at him curiously. But that was enough for him. It was sufficient to have someone to whom he could express his inexpressible sorrow. When he dragged his feet home, the dog would slowly get up and follow a little way behind him, its tail and head bowed.

Finally the day came when his parents decided on a divorce, and his mother gathered her two children to return to Kōbe, where her sister and brother-in-law lived. It was May, when the rows of street-side acacia trees unique to Dalian were in full bloom, their white petals fluttering in the wind and skittering to the pavement. When he climbed into the horse carriage packed with suitcases and wicker trunks, he looked back at the familiar house, only to realize that his dog was standing despondently at the gate looking towards him. When the Manchurian driver gave a lethargic flick of his whip and the carriage jerked forward, the dog chased after it for five or six paces, then stopped in resignation. That was the last he saw of his dog.

The dog had been named Blackie. After he grew up, Chiba always had a dog around the house. Not a Western dog or a dog with a certificate of pedigree, but a mongrel no better than a stray, one that would remind him of his original Blackie, who had stared at him in the Dalian park buried in dead leaves that nightfall in late autumn.

After he got married, Chiba frequently argued with his wife

over his dogs. She had never been fond of animals, and early in their marriage she could not stand having him bring his dog into the house on rainy days, or watching him deliberately leave portions of the food she had gone to the trouble to cook so that he could give them to the dog.

'Try putting yourself in the place of the person who has to do the cleaning around here. I can't stand all the hair it leaves by the door, and all the mess it makes.'

'It's a living thing. It can't help it!' he yelled. 'Even a dog gets cold on rainy nights. Fine. Starting tomorrow, I'll clean the entryway.'

He was, however, unable to stick to his vow longer than two days. His wife criticized him for being wilful in his attachment to the dog, and while this debate continued to rage between them year after year he ended up keeping a mongrel at his house. His current pet, Whitey, he had discovered in a box with his siblings in front of the dairy one spring evening thirteen years ago while he was out taking a walk.

One day late in autumn, while he was working at home, he heard Whitey coughing strangely.

'What do you suppose that cough is?'

'I imagine he has a cold,' his wife answered indifferently. 'He's been doing that for some time now.'

'Why didn't you say anything?'

'Well, why should I say anything just because he's coughing? He's getting old, you know.'

Chiba put on his garden shoes and went out to the doghouse. Whitey was crouched down in front of his aluminium water dish. When he saw his owner, he gave a dutiful wag of his tail, but he also emitted two or three unpleasantly dry hacking coughs. Because some thirteen years had passed since he had acquired this dog, in human terms he was an old man of seventy-five. When Whitey had reached approximately the same age as his owner, every time Chiba came home drunk he would go out into the rear garden and pat the dog's head and encourage him by saying: 'Hey, my friend, we both have our share of problems, don't we?' And when the dog got older, he

jested: 'Well, Grandpa, let's keep up the good fight together.'
Now the dog had pulled away from him in age and become
truly elderly. He lay constantly basking in the sun, and he
staggered when he walked; it also seemed he had grown rather
deaf, since he would not open his eyes unless you made a fairly
loud noise.

'What's the matter?'
As he gently patted the dog's chin, he looked at the pond in
his garden. The water, which he did virtually nothing to look
after, was a murky black, and a potted lotus plant had finally
begun to send its stalks in all directions, displaying brown
buds. In the shade of one of those buds, a goldfish lay dead. He
had been breeding goldfish in the pond for two or three years.
Unlike with the dog, he didn't have to do anything for the fish
except feed them occasionally. He thought perhaps some con-
taminated water had seeped into the pond, but there was no
sign that such was the case. Perhaps it had simply lived out its
appointed life-span.

Floating belly-up, the stomach of the goldfish was oddly
puffy. Its scales, once golden, had turned white, perhaps because two or three days had passed since its death. Chiba
suddenly remembered a friend remarking that the only living
creature that didn't exude a sense of death was a killifish.
Rather than being impressed by the comment, Chiba was struck
by how old his friend had grown, so sensitive had he become to
the death of inconsequential creatures.

'We're both getting old, aren't we?' He attached the leash to
his dog's collar and set out. Whitey could no longer walk at the
same nimble pace as when he was young. He faltered a bit, the
only sign of energy his agitated breathing, as he slowly ambled
ahead of Chiba. From time to time he sniffed at scents along the
roadside, halted and urinated a few drops, and then made that
loathsome cough.

He took Whitey to the little veterinary clinic where he always
got his rabies injections. The young veterinarian had rolled up
the sleeves of his sports shirt, and sat in the empty examination-room browsing through a comic book with the drawing of

a nude woman on the cover.

'I'd better take a blood sample. He may have filaria again.'

Filaria, which most dogs contract from mosquitoes, was just what Chiba had feared might be the problem. Ordinarily dogs were given an annual vaccination against the disease, but such a potent medication could not be administered to a dog as old as Whitey.

Suddenly hoisted on to the examination table, Whitey gave Chiba a piteous look. He resembled a pathetic old man who's been dragged off to the doctor by his relatives and forced to strip naked. He and the doctor restrained the dog, telling him: 'It's all right, it's all right.' When the doctor poked a needle into his rump, Whitey howled as if to say 'That hurts!'

'He has filaria again after all,' the young doctor mumbled as he peered through his microscope. 'I can't use the strong medicine because of his age. He's really become quite infirm.'

'About how long does a dog usually live?'

'Normally around ten years. So your dog has survived quite a long while. I know one dog who lived to twenty, but he was an indoor pet.'

'Very well, then, I'm going to see to it that Whitey lives twenty years and gets appointed an honorary citizen of this town. You'll recommend him, won't you, doctor?' Chiba threw in his routine jest.

The old dog still looked frightened and pitiful as Chiba led him home, and he remembered the spring day when he had first set eyes on Whitey. A cardboard box had been placed in a sunny spot in front of the dairy, and four puppies peered out from it. As he passed by, Chiba unwittingly stopped and gaped inside. A white ball of wool came crawling towards him, and when he looked at it more closely, one of its eyes, caked with mucus, was clenched shut. Still the one-eyed puppy wagged its tail so furiously it seemed as if it would fly off at any moment.

'You can have one for nothing. Any one you like,' the dairyman called out. 'That one's no good. One of his eyes won't open.'

Chiba smiled. 'That's why I want him. Can I have him?'

And so Chiba took Whitey into his home. Once again his wife looked annoyed, but several doses of liver oil cured the puppy's eye.

'I can't take it any more. It's no good as a watch-dog and it does nothing but make trouble for me.'

Whitey provided a constant source of bickering between husband and wife. It was true that this kind of dog was so friendly it wouldn't bark when a pushy salesman came to the door, but would welcome him with wagging tail. When Chiba took him out for a stroll, he would suddenly stop in front of some stranger's house and drop a load, or he might slip out of his collar and run away and not come back for two or three days. On those occasions, invariably they would receive a complaining telephone call. Someone would protest that Chiba's dog had made strange moves on their foreign-bred hound. Every time they got one of those calls, Chiba repeatedly bowed his head into the receiver apologetically.

'If you're going to have a dog anyway, could you please get one a bit brighter? That idiot dog's of no use to anybody.'

'Are you telling me we ought to get rid of him if he's no use?'

From the garden, Whitey watched dolefully through the glass door as Chiba and his wife bickered. Being the kind of man he was, Chiba was irritated by his wife's contention that something was unbearable because it was of no practical use. Once he had bought a used Austin and driven it. For a couple of years the second-hand car had served him and his wife and family quite well. When they all crammed into the car and tried driving up a hill, the vehicle would wheeze, as though it were panting, even asthmatic.

One day, when his wife proposed, 'Dear, why don't we get rid of this old clunker and buy a new car?', Chiba got truly angry. For some time now he had felt as if that car, which breathlessly climbed the hills transporting his entire family, was the very image of himself. He stubbornly rejected his wife's suggestion, and once again had a row with her.

'Who gives a damn about raising some foreign dog? Isn't that right, Whitey?' When the quarrel was over, Chiba went out into the garden, and just as he had done in Dalian in late autumn, he spoke his heart only to his dog. Whitey lowered his head as though abashed, and licked his master's hand.

'What's someone of your age doing trying to learn ballroom dancing?'

Whenever one of his friends taunted him in this manner, Chiba would jokingly respond: 'Dancing's the only time someone my age can freely put his arms around a young woman.'

At rehearsals, of course, during the two hours or so that they were drilled in the complicated steps of the dance, he never had the leisure to sense the woman in his partner. At those times, Mimi-chan and the other women who danced with him became no more than accessories to the dance, like the music or his patent-leather shoes.

'Mr Chiba, move the lower part of your body in closer. You've got to thrust in right between her legs.'

When the teacher shouted these directions, which might have been taken to mean something different in other circumstances, no one laughed, and not even Chiba thought it strange. Even when Chiba jabbed his thigh between the young woman's legs he felt nothing whatsoever. Once he had finally pounded the complex steps into his head, however, he secretly began to savour the smell of sweat emitted by the body of this woman young enough to be his daughter.

As they waltzed or tangoed, circling the floor of the classroom-cum-ballroom two or three times before the music stopped, a stream of sweat trickled down nineteen-year-old Mimi-chan's neck. Her pulsating flesh blushed a faint red, and he smelled the faint aroma of sweat undiluted by perfume. This was not a neck or chin globbed with flesh and rippled with wrinkles like his wife's; and, making sure the teacher did not notice, he quietly inhaled the smell of the young woman's sweat, and thrilled to a momentary sensation not unlike vertigo. And the thought that always came to him after that attack of dizziness had gone was that he was an old man past the age of fifty.

As he came to feel at home on the dance-floor, he got caught up in a variety of fantasies as he watched the teacher and the others dancing. When the teacher and his partner demonstrated the tango, they shook their heads and bodies violently. That reminded Chiba of the convulsions of intercourse, and the way Mimi-chan tilted her head and stared vacantly off into space when they waltzed together made him think of the look on the faces of young women truly in love. When he danced with a partner who had no interest in him, the way she moved her legs seemed slapdash, and there was a hardness to the way she used her hands. Nearly a year had passed since they had started learning to dance, and Chiba was able to guess from the way the women danced just how much of a sense of intimacy had developed between the various men and women of the group, and the fluctuations of their hearts.

He naturally said nothing about any of this. He kept secret the thoughts that passed through a fifty-year-old man's mind as he inhaled Mimi-chan's sweat. When they had finished dancing, he joined the others in putting the chairs and desks back in place in the classroom, and then walked down the empty hallway and out through the door. When they reached the main road, he bid farewell to the young people who were going off for a drink, and they bowed to him and said goodbye.

As summer approached, Whitey's cough grew worse. The veterinarian, noting that it would have little effect since he couldn't use the more potent injections, gave Chiba some liquid medicine to pour down the dog's throat. Whitey slept beneath the shade of a tree nearly all day long, and once in a while he would get up and stagger over to the pond, where he drank the blackened water and coughed. On the surface of the pond one lotus flower had bloomed in the sultry heat.

One sweltering morning, Chiba was abruptly awakened by his wife.

'Get up! Your brother's in a critical condition!'

From his bed Chiba looked up blearily at his wife's round face. His head was still fuzzy, and the vibrant image of his only brother did not mesh in his mind with the words 'critical condition'. 'What nonsense are you talking?' he quietly mumbled to his wife.

He jammed his feet into his shoes and raced ahead of his wife out into the street. The taxis that ordinarily passed by here with annoying frequency were nowhere to be seen. The broad street that early morning was vacant, and several blue plastic buckets were lined in front of stores still closed for business. The taxi they were finally able to hail somehow seemed to have no speed, and stopped lethargically at every red traffic light. At one of those signals, he remembered that he had been out romping the night his mother collapsed with a stroke, and that he had not been there at the moment she died.

In the hospital corridor, his two nieces were weeping. Through their sobs, they told him that early in the morning their father had suddenly vomited up an enormous quantity of blood, and twice in his room since he was taken to the hospital he had again coughed up a great deal of blood. Blackish bloodstains still blotched the floor of his room here and there. Large graphs of blood soiled the several towels that had been rolled up in a ball and placed under the wash-basin. Two doctors, two nurses and his sister-in-law surrounded his brother's body as if to protect it, and transfusion bags and an oxygen tank flanked the bed. When an elderly doctor realized that the patient's younger brother had arrived, he signalled with his eyes and accompanied Chiba out into the corridor.

'A vein in his oesophagus ruptured,' the doctor explained, pointing to his own throat. A lump had developed on the blood vessels in his oesophagus and, when that ruptured, blood had come gushing out uncontrollably.

'I've inserted an ice-pack in his oesophagus as an emergency measure. But if I keep it there the whole day, the membranes in his oesophagus will be destroyed. I'm eventually going to have to remove the ice-pack.'

'After you remove it . . . what will happen?'

'He will probably . . . vomit up blood again.'

'Then . . . we're looking at surgery?'

'Yes. But very few of these kinds of operations are performed in the entire world. There is one doctor at A. University who performs it, but. . . .' The old doctor looked searchingly into Chiba's eyes. Chiba had a clear grasp of his unspoken meaning. The operation was extremely dangerous; but there was no hope for his brother except through surgery.

'There's no other way?'

'I'm sorry, but there isn't.'

'Then please go ahead. Will the doctor from A. University come?' His brother's son had not yet arrived, so Chiba spoke in his stead. Chiba's nephew worked at a broadcast network in Hamamatsu, and hearing of the crisis he was now hurrying to the hospital. Until he arrived, the responsibility for making this decision rested solely with Chiba.

He stood beside his brother's pillow; rubber tubes and needles had been stabbed into his body. The patient had lost six pints of blood, and his unfocused eyes were trained on the ceiling. He didn't seem to know that his younger brother had come. A nurse repeatedly checked his blood pressure, and the doctor listened to his weakening heart.

Not once had Chiba considered the possibility that his brother, only three years older than himself, might ever be stricken by such an unexpected calamity. He had always thought that his brother, who was his superior in all respects, would likewise live much longer than he. He had no idea how to cope with the fact that this brother was now on the verge of dying. His intelligent, serious-minded brother had attained a considerable position in society, but that meant nothing to Chiba. For him, his brother was the person who had shared in his youthful grief that cold late autumn in Dalian when their parents had become estranged. Unlike Chiba, who had dawdled outside, not want-ing to see his mother's grim face as she sat motionless in her room, his brother, he knew, had endured the situation by sitting at his desk and opening his school-books. Once they were separated from their father, the two brothers had endured many trials they could not express to outsiders, but they knew of each other's pain as intimately as if they had been twins. 'I'm not going to let you die,' Chiba muttered to himself, and left the room.

His wife, who had been sitting alone in a hallway chair, came up to him. 'He's in danger,' he reported, 'but they're going to operate. If they don't save him, I'll end up an orphan.'

She gave him a tearful smile and muttered: 'An orphan means a little child. You really don't know anything about how to use words, do you?'

'There's no telling when I'll end up like this.'

'Don't be silly. You're only just over fifty.'

That's true, he nodded, and walked over to the pay telephone at the end of the corridor. Because they'd raced out of the house so early that morning, there were a number of things he had to report to the housekeeper.

'Any problems?'

'Whitey is acting strangely,' the housekeeper reported. 'He just lies there and won't move at all. His breathing is very heavy, too.'

'Did you call the vet? Call him immediately and have him come over. Immediately!'

He went back to his chair and told his wife that Whitey was dying, but she said nothing. 'Whitey's critical, too,' he repeated. 'Did you hear me?'

'So what if he is? Your brother is the important one.'

His brother was important, of course, but for Chiba Whitey was important too. He started to tell his wife that, but checked himself. His wife knew nothing about the mongrel that had stared at him in the park at Dalian so many years before.

Chiba returned home exhausted the next morning. During the eight-hour operation, he had waited in the hospital room with his brother's family, and then taken turns sitting in the bedside chair and dozing off. When he got home he didn't even speak to the housekeeper but went directly out into the garden. Whitey was lying on his side outside the doghouse, his legs outstretched and his eyes open a crack. His abdomen heaved repeatedly and his breathing was laboured. When he saw his master through narrowed eyelids, he made a desperate effort to wag his tail, but he could not stand up.

'It's all right. It's all right.' Chiba stroked the dog's stomach. 'You don't have to wag your tail.'

The single goldfish still floated upside-down, dead in the murky black water of the pond. Its belly, which had turned white, was weirdly swollen. The dead goldfish floating in the water looked very much like Whitey lying on his side.

The veterinarian came. He poked two thick needles into the dog's rump, which was caked with mud, but the animal no longer had the strength to cry out.

'Will he make it?'

'I'm not sure. He's old, after all. You had better resign yourself to the fact that his time has come.'

'Please do whatever you can.'

'Uh-huh,' the young veterinarian equivocated, with no confidence in his answer. 'I'll do everything possible, but. . . .'

After the doctor left, Chiba picked up Whitey so that he could put him down in the shade where a cool breeze blew. In his arms the sick dog was heavy as a stone. After putting the animal in the shade, he opened its mouth with his fingers and tried squirting some milk between the pink gums with a dropper, but the white liquid dribbled uselessly down the dog's whiskers and on to Chiba's knee.

The sun felt hot. An unsightly growth of weeds surrounded the half-opened cosmos blossoms. Chiba crouched for a long while beside his ailing dog. The dog stretched his four legs out horizontally along the ground, and with his eyes open only a crack lay there motionless. As he gazed at the cosmos flowers, Chiba thought of how many people, how many living things he had encountered in his day. But the people with whom he had truly had some connection, and the living things with which he had had a true bond, were few indeed. His dead mother. His elder brother in the hospital. And the cross-breed dog that had watched him in the park. Certainly Whitey, who had lived with him for thirteen years, had been closely tied to his life. The stems of the cosmos fluttered faintly in the wind, and a single greenbottle fly lighted on the dog's chin. By then, Whitey was already dead. His eyes remained open a crack as they had just moments before, but the abdomen that had struggled for breath was at rest, and around his whiskers the milk that Chiba had squirted into the dog's mouth had dried whitely on his whiskers. As his fingers passed over Whitey's eyelids, Chiba wept.

Sensing what had happened, his wife stepped down into the garden and crouched beside him quietly for a few moments. Then she bleakly muttered: 'He died in place of your brother.' Then she plucked several cosmos flowers and laid them on Whitey's head.

At nightfall, after placing sticks of incense and flowers around Whitey's body, they hurried to the hospital. The patient still lay sound asleep behind a transparent vinyl tent, surrounded by oxygen tanks and transfusion bottles, but his breathing was more regular than Chiba had expected. As the old doctor at the bedside put away his stethoscope, he whispered that if Chiba's brother could maintain his present condition until the following evening, there was hope for him. When Chiba heard those words, exhaustion overtook him in an instant, and he sat down in a chair in the corridor. Once again a headache coursed through the back of his head like ink dropped into water. When he closed his eyes, he remembered his wife saying that Whitey had died in his brother's place. I'll make a grave for you in a flower garden, he told Whitey.

Japanese in Warsaw

That evening large, fleecy clouds danced over the Warsaw airport. About ten Japanese disembarked from the Polish Airlines flight that had just landed. Compared with the Poles on the flight, who wore fur hats and were fully braced against the winter cold, the company of Japanese stood out conspicuously with their shoulders frigidly hunched, cameras dangling from their necks, and the Japan Airlines bags with their distinctive crane designs. They clustered together by themselves at the back of the queue waiting to pass through immigration, nervously holding out their passports.

Suddenly, from amongst the throng gathered to welcome the arrivals, a young Japanese man wearing a ski-cap and woollen gloves called out: 'Are you with Mr Tamura's party? I'm Shimizu, of the Orbis Travel Bureau. I'm here to meet you.'

'Hey, somebody's come to meet us,' one of the Japanese yelled out.

The other foreigners turned round in surprise at the loudness of his voice.

'What a relief! We'd have been goners for sure if somebody wasn't here to meet us.'

'How strict are the Customs people here?'

'They're very strict when it comes to declaring how much money you're bringing in, but at Customs they'll probably search only one of you.'

After they passed through immigration, Shimizu led the Japanese group *en masse* to Customs, where they began unlocking their luggage. The Customs agent, wearing a uniform resembling that of a policeman, extracted a tin of dried seaweed from one suitcase and asked in English what it was. The Japanese man gestured with both hands to suggest that he was eating, and answered: 'Ea-to. Ea-to.' After Shimizu explained in Polish, the agent drew a circle with white chalk on the suitcase. When the Customs inspection was finished, the Japanese walked to the rented coach that was waiting for them outside in the cold.

In the faint light of dusk, as they raced along the motorway leading directly into the city, the scene that stretched out before their eyes through the windows on one side of the bus was of a vast expanse of snow splotched with dark-purple shadows. Far in the distance, beneath a gloomy sky, the city of Warsaw looked frigid and forlorn.

'This is really depressing. It's very different from Paris, Mr Shimizu.'

'Warsaw was brutally damaged during the war.' Shimizu answered dutifully, not even turning round in his seat near the driver. He didn't seem to feel a jot of intimacy or fondness towards his fellow-countrymen.

'How many years have you lived here?' Tamura asked.

'Two years.'

'Is this a part-time job? Are you a student?'

'Yes, I am.'

As the coach pulled into Warsaw, tired-looking men and women wearing fur hats were hurrying home from work along pavements sullied with mud and snow. There was a screeching noise when a run-down tram turned the corner. A long queue of people waited patiently at the tram-stop.

'It's desolate. There's hardly a neon sign anywhere.'

'This is Saski Plaza,' Shimizu reported without expression. 'Your hotel, the Europejski, is on this plaza.'

The coach slowly circled the darkened square. It stopped in front of a dilapidated, nineteenth-century-style building that looked imposing only on the exterior, and two porters from the hotel, dressed in gold-braided uniforms, came out to welcome them.

'I'll handle all the arrangements, so please let me have your passports. It will take some time to complete the paperwork, so please take a seat in the lobby.' Standing in front of the revolving door at the hotel entrance, Shimizu collected passports from each of the ten Japanese as they got off the coach, then went alone to the front desk to arrange the room allocations.

'We shouldn't have come here.' The Japanese sat down and looked anxiously around the dimly lit, deserted lobby, which had nothing more to offer than an inordinately high ceiling. The only sound from the front desk was the tapping of typewriter keys. Two or three of the men went to have a look at the gift shop in the far corner, but they came back with sneers on their faces.

'No good. No good. Nothing worth buying. I have no idea what kind of souvenirs to get from this place.'

'Women. This is one of those great places for women nobody knows about.' Tamura, who seemed to be the leader of the group, sought to encourage his downcast comrades. 'That's why we came here. Isn't that right, Imamiya?'

Imamiya was flicking the Dupont lighter he had bought in Paris, while his eyes followed two young women who had just come into the hotel. Both women were tall and blonde. The men had come here because they had heard there were many beautiful women in Poland, and the sight of these two confirmed that report. During this foreign excursion Imamiya had paid for women in London and Paris, but none of them were to his satisfaction. As co-workers in the same industry these men had travelled overseas on the pretext of observing factory operations, but Imamiya, like the other Japanese, had conjured up private goals unrelated to factory observation: to buy a lot of things and to dally with a lot of women.

Once the rooms were assigned and the keys handed over, the group climbed to the second floor and turned the knobs of the doors to the rooms where they would be staying in groups of two. Each room was so dismal, with a hard bed and a torn shade on the bedside light, that they wondered if this was truly a first-class hotel for Warsaw. The wash-basin in the bathroom was black with grime, and the drain in the tub was revoltingly rusted. When they turned on the hot water to test it, it came out a murky red colour, obviously not something they wanted to use. Imamiya, who had teamed up with Tamura, noticed with alarm how coarse and stiff the toilet-paper was. He suffered from haemorrhoids and had to use soft tissue.

'Tamura, did you bring some tissue paper?'

'I did. Why?' He looked over suspiciously from the bed where he sat, pulling from his bags the bottles of antacid and cold medication he had brought from Japan.

'Take a look in the toilet. I don't know of any country these days that uses such toilet-paper.'

The city reminded Imamiya of Changchun in Manchuria. As a soldier during the war he had been in Changchun briefly. Like Warsaw, in Changchun even the pavements in the bustling downtown region were smudged with mud and snow, and he remembered that all the Japanese walking along the streets had their faces and ears covered to ward off the cold.

'You're right.' Tamura had poked his head in the bathroom and returned with a sullen face. 'This is awful.' But since he was the one who had encouraged his friends to come to Warsaw, he had to mutter as if to himself: 'But, after all, this will give us something to talk about when we get home.'

After they had checked out the rooms, the men assembled once again in the vacant lobby, and at Shimizu's suggestion they went to the restaurant on the same floor. But it seemed less like a hotel restaurant than a wretched dance-hall, where two or three groups of foreign guests hunched over their plates and ate insipid food with knives and forks. In the corner a tiny band played a perfunctory waltz. Not one person applauded when they finished a number. As the men blithely slurped away at the soup they ordered, grumbling all the while about the miserable rooms in the hotel, Shimizu flipped through the pages of his itinerary.

'Tomorrow at 10 a.m. the city tour bus will pick you up at the hotel,' he announced.

'You expect us just to go to sleep like this tonight?'

'Women, is it? If it's women you want, you can pick them up in the snack-bar here in the hotel, but you can't take them to your rooms. The police are an awful nuisance, so be careful. The women will take you to their own apartments.' Shimizu spewed the words out in a monotone voice, as though he were reciting a memorized speech. He had been working part-time for the tour company for a year, but he had to provide the same information to the few groups of Japanese tourists who came to Poland. Again today he had to give the identical explanation in identical words. He knew that this was the only time they would listen to him carefully, staring into his face like obedient schoolchildren.

'But how do we get back here? Can we find taxis?'

'There are some taxis, but if you ask the woman she'll call one for you. Some women will even bring you here in their own cars.'

'Well, how considerate!' Tamura proudly looked around at the others. 'I told you how good Warsaw was!'

Once the subject of women came up, some life finally infused the stagnant air. After dinner, in high spirits they closed ranks and waddled in single file like ducks towards the snack-bar on the same floor of the hotel. When the invading force of Japanese entered the crowded snack-bar, the Poles who had been enjoying a light meal abruptly broke off their conversations.

'Mr Shimizu. Which women are we talking about?'

'They're scattered everywhere. Generally if a woman is having a beer by herself, she's one of them. They'll signal you with their eyes, so you'll know. Then I'll do the negotiating.'

Shimizu recalled that he had said exactly the same thing in precisely the same spot just three months earlier to a Japanese professor from a state university. Shimizu had seen the name of this professor, who had come to attend an international conference held in Warsaw, in Japanese newspapers and magazines. After the conference he went out of his way to exchange hugs and name-cards with the Polish scholars who had shared the podium with him, while meanwhile he was sending Shimizu, whom he treated like a research assistant, on all sorts of errands. The evening before his departure, he surprised Shimizu by inviting him to the snack-bar and having a few drinks with him. But when he suddenly smiled thinly and asked Shimizu to find him a woman for the night, Shimizu felt nothing but contempt for the man.

Over the year he had been guiding Japanese tourists for the travel company, Shimizu had gradually determined that he would turn himself into a sort of machine. A machine that would welcome them at the airport, and see them off at the airport. A machine that would check them into the hotel, and get their room allocations for them. A machine that would translate for shopping and sightseeing. A machine that would take them to taverns and snack-bars where they could meet women. A machine that would listen as they ridiculed the poverty of Poland. A machine that would never let its own thoughts or feelings show on its face. Had he not become such a machine, he could never have done this pimp-like work for Japanese tourists. When their stay was ended and he delivered them to the airport, once he had bowed his head and wished them a safe trip at the gate, he never had to deal with them again for his entire life. Not one tourist had ever sent him a single letter or even a postcard to thank him for his assistance. They had merely used Shimizu as a convenient tool during their brief stay overseas.

Half an hour later eight of the men had found companions for the night. Shimizu asked the two remaining men if they wanted to go to a bar in town to look for a woman. They looked at one another and said they would give it up for tonight. Shimizu felt relieved. Imamiya was one of the leftovers.

When the other eight Japanese had headed off for various hotels with their women, Imamiya walked through the empty lobby and went back to the room he shared with Tamura, where he ran some bath-water. He wondered if the water, which was brown when it first came out of the tap, would eventually clear up. But though there seemed to be less rust the more water he ran, it never did clear entirely. Stoically he climbed into the tub, and after bathing he rinsed out his underpants. He had few regrets that he had not been able to frolic with a woman that night. Only two days before he came to Warsaw, a prostitute at the place de la Concorde in Paris had called to him from her car. Her dog sat in the passenger seat as she drove him to a cheap hotel next to the opera-house. Unlike his youthful days, he had reached an age when he no longer wanted a woman every night. And he had realized after several experiences that foreign women were not as he had imagined them while he was in Japan. The skin of their bellies and thighs was rough and scratchy as bark, and sometimes, thanks to the dark illumination in the assignation-rooms, their faces looked like demons. The moment the woman he had picked up in the Concorde stepped into the room she headed for the bathroom, where the sound of her urinating thoroughly revolted Imamiya as he sat listening through the door.

He put on his dressing-gown and took out a fountain-pen to write on the remaining postcards he had bought in France. He wrote to his daughter and her husband in Nagasaki that he had found the distinctive eau-de-Cologne and perfume they had requested. In his youth Imamiya had lived in Nagasaki, and his daughter had married into a family that had been close to his parents there. So, although he had lived in Osaka now for forty years, when he was drunk or perplexed the words that tumbled from his mouth were sometimes in the Nagasaki dialect.

He finished writing his postcards and lay down on the bed. The mattress was as hard as a steel plate.

The next morning, as the Japanese were climbing on to the sightseeing coach that had come to pick them up, a single platoon of soldiers had begun to form ranks on the Saski Plaza in front of the hotel. When Shimizu explained that every Sunday a military parade was held at the Tomb of the Unknown Soldier on this plaza, four or five of the Japanese quickly slung cameras over their necks and went racing out to the plaza still buried in snow. While the remaining Japanese watched from the bus with eyes hollow from lack of sleep, to the blare of a trumpet the soldiers raised their rifles with fixed bayonets to their shoulders and began to march, kicking away the snow. For a time snow continued to fall on the parade, then finally it stopped.

Half an hour behind schedule, the coach set out towards the Wisła River that runs through the city. Beside the driver's seat Shimizu tested his microphone and then began his exposition on the sights.

'The city of Warsaw that you are about to see may still seem to have much of the flavour of a city of old about it. You may think, when you see the medieval-style houses, the stone-paved plazas and the baroque buildings, that each has survived from former times, but in fact they were all constructed after the war. The Nazis, who occupied Warsaw in 1939, utterly destroyed the city at Hitler's command. Hitler ordered his underlings to remove the city and even the name of Warsaw from the map of the world for all eternity. The destruction was so complete that it was thought impossible that the city, which had been reduced to a mountain of bricks, could be rebuilt in even a hundred years. But after the war the people of Warsaw, relying on old sketches of the city, one by one carried stones, piled up bricks, and restored Warsaw just as it had been, from the colour of the walls to the shapes of the doors.'

Shimizu had repeated this speech many times over to Japanese tourists. He recited the canned commentary again today, and waited for the gasps of amazement. Before long, those exclamations echoed through the coach. The way in which the Japanese hurriedly turned their cameras to the window was always the same. Shutters clicked here and there.

'We are now driving through Zamkowy Plaza, also known as the Royal Castle Square. The bronze statue of Sigismund III, which stands in the middle of the square, and the Gothic Cathedral of St John have been reconstructed as they were before they were destroyed by German troops. The wounds of war still cut deep here in Poland, and the Polish people have not yet forgotten the scars inflicted on them by the German and Soviet armies. As you know, Poland is unquestionably a communist country, but a unique feature of this country is that ninety per cent of the population are simultaneously members of the Catholic Church. Communism and Christianity coexist in this land.'

This time nobody was listening. All he could hear was the shutter of a camera clicking on the right side of the coach. Oblivious to the interests of the Japanese tourists, Shimizu like a tape-recorder continued his commentary in a prosaic voice. He knew full well that not one of these Japanese sightseers had any interest in or curiosity about the commingling of communism and Christianity. It was part of Shimizu's subtle revenge on the Japanese tourists that he purposely droned on and on about the Polish Communist Party and the Church while knowing full well they were uninterested. It was his intangible retribution against fellow-countrymen who made him procure women for them along with everything else.

'I'm so sleepy.' Seated beside Imamiya, Tamura peered out of the bus window with puffy eyes. 'It was almost dawn when I came back to the hotel, you know. How was it? It was quite good. The women here have feeling. It's not just a business for them, they're providing a service for you.'

Before long Tamura's head collapsed clumsily against the window as he fell asleep. He was not alone; three or four other men had dropped off in their seats.

'To your right is Warsaw University. In former days this was the palace of the King of Poland.' Shimizu continued to talk into the microphone as if he were unaware of the dozing passengers. 'On the university campus the house where Chopin once lived is being used for classrooms.'

The spots where the Japanese took pictures were always predictable. The statue of the mermaid that stood on the banks of the Wisła River. The remains of the Jewish ghetto in the Muranów district. The bronze statue of Copernicus. Although many of them were sound asleep on the coach, once he mentioned these spots that appeared on postcards, they made the coach stop and charged out, scrambling to be the first to point their cameras in the appropriate direction. Once they had made the rounds of the famous tourist sites, they would return to the

Miasto market in the old part of the city, where they would have lunch. Then Shimizu would assist them in their shopping, after which they had free time until the evening.

When they reached the old city market some two hours later, Shimizu advised the group: 'We have just arrived at Miasto Plaza, the most beautiful square in all of Warsaw. There are many souvenir shops here, so feel free to buy whatever you wish. Please have lunch on your own here.'

As soon as the Japanese got off the coach, however, they flocked together and walked round the square. Several other tour coaches had parked on the stone pavement where frosty snow lingered like tiny sand-bars after the ebb tide, and tourists were peering into the surrounding souvenir shops. Nearly all the shops sold folk crafts, dolls dressed in native costumes and hand-woven fabrics. In disappointment someone remarked: 'These are all just childish trinkets. Isn't there any better stuff, Mr Shimizu?'

'Would you like to go to an antique shop? But the government won't allow the really good items to be taken out of the country.'

Like a group of scouts following their leader, the men refused to leave Shimizu's side. When one bought a doll, another bought a doll; when one took a look at some fabric, someone else examined fabric.

While the young female clerk was wrapping the doll Tamura bought, she smiled and began saying something to him. Since Tamura could understand no Polish, he turned to Shimizu and asked: 'What's she saying?'

'She's asking, since you're Japanese, you must know Father Kolbe.'

'Who's he?'

'He's the Christian Father most revered by the Polish people.'

'I don't know any of those "Amen" fellows.'

When Tamura waved his hand to answer 'No, no', the clerk nodded, but she looked rather saddened.

At the same shop Imamiya bought his youngest daughter, who was attending the university, a tapestry depicting a Polish farm woman. In London and Paris as well he had diligently cast about for souvenirs for his family, and had purchased a watch and a handbag for his wife. Every time he went back to his hotel room and placed a souvenir in his suitcase, Imamiya thought of himself as a good family man.

Although there was no reason why the men could not have had lunch or taken a walk separately, not one of them engaged in any activity apart from the rest, so they all ordered lunch at the same restaurant. The shop was famous for its shellfish and its excellent Polish meat dish known as *bigos*, and the Johnny Walker turned up the volume of the Japanese men's already boisterous voices. Tamura, his face a bright red, raised his glass of Johnny Walker to toast the Polish man quietly eating in the next seat. The middle-aged Pole, who looked like an office worker, smiled back and said: 'You're from the country where Father Kolbe worked, aren't you?'

'Again!' Exasperated, Tamura asked Shimizu: 'Kolbe. Just who is this Kolbe fellow?'

Without expression, Shimizu answered: 'Let's have him tell you.'

During his two years in Poland, Shimizu himself had heard the story of Father Kolbe over and over again from various people. But instead of telling the story himself, he deliberately asked the Polish man in the neighbouring seat, because he didn't want to offer any more than the essential service to his countrymen, and because he wanted to continue to function as a machine. The middle-aged Pole, dressed in an old, threadbare suit, continued to clutch his knife and fork as he nodded at Shimizu's questions.

'In 1941 Father Kolbe was confined in the Auschwitz internment camp for harbouring anti-Nazi sentiments. I think you all must have heard about this camp, where mass slaughters were carried out by means of forced labour and gas. The priest was suffering from tuberculosis, but he kept that to himself, and for three months he and the other captives were forced to dispose of the corpses from the gas chamber in that infernal prison.' Each time the Pole paused in his explanation Shimizu closed his eyes and translated in a lifeless voice. 'Three months later a prisoner escaped from the camp. The commandant placed the responsibility for the escape on all the prisoners, and as a warning he chose ten of them and put them in the hunger bunker.'

'What's a "hunger bunker"?'

Without any expression on his face, Shimizu relayed the question to the Polish man.

'A hunger bunker? It's a room where the people were kept in isolation, without bread or even a drop of water, until they died. There was another tiny execution chamber at Auschwitz, called the suffocation bunker. Many people were put in there, and the door was not opened until they had run out of oxygen and died.' The Pole's mouth twisted. 'On the day the prisoner escaped, the commandant made all the prisoners stand outside through the night, and then he chose the ten who were to be punished. One of them was a man named Gajowniczek. When his name was called, Gajowniczek began to weep at the thought of his wife and children. Just then a man stepped forward. It was Father Kolbe. He stood before the commandant and asked to be placed in the hunger bunker in place of Gajowniczek. Unlike this man, he said, I am a priest, and I have no wife or children. The commandant granted his request, and he was thrown into the subterranean chamber along with the other nine. Granted not even a cup of water, over a period of two weeks the captives began to die of starvation one after another, until only the priest and four other men remained alive. They were killed by a Nazi doctor who injected them with carbolic acid.'

It was silent inside the well-heated restaurant, and for a time the Japanese said nothing. Finally one of them muttered forlornly: 'What a horrid story!'

Suddenly the Pole remarked: 'Please go to Auschwitz while you're here.' Shimizu relayed this comment to the Japanese with the same blank look, but Tamura spoke for all when he shook his head and said: 'We're not going. Warsaw has been more than enough.' The Pole did not respond, but peered at the Japanese with dejected eyes.

'Dziękuję.' Shimizu thanked the man. 'Shall we head back to the coach?'

Relieved, the Japanese noisily rose from their chairs. With a cigarette dangling from his lips, Tamura called out from behind Shimizu: 'What's this Kolbe fellow got to do with Japan?'

'He spent two years as a missionary in Nagasaki.'

'What? Really? When was that?'

'I understand it was around 1930 or 1931.'

That afternoon there were still several tour coaches parked in the square, but perhaps because it was lunch-time they were deserted. Thanks to the sun seeping between the clouds, the muddy, icy snow began to melt. Walking alongside the others and carrying his sack of souvenirs, Imamiya thought back on the several foreign missionaries he had met in the streets of Nagasaki as he commuted to elementary school around 1930. At the time, the Imamiya house had stood on the slope leading to Ōura, and his father had operated a transport business. There in Ōura, which had been a foreign residential district since the early days of the Meiji period, it was not at all unusual to see foreigners climbing and descending the stone-paved hill. A number of foreign missionaries lived at the Ōura Catholic church and, dressed in their frocks, companies of them would often pass in front of the Imamiya house. Rumour had it that they had converted an abandoned Western-style house near the cathedral into a printing plant, where they published Bibles and prayer-books.

Whenever Imamiya ran into those missionaries on the hill, he, like the other children, would run and hide. He was frightened and apprehensive of the foreign missionaries who sported chin whiskers and wore long, peculiar black robes.

Kudō, a printer who came calling at his father's shop one day, remarked: 'Those men eat wretched food.' He had worked for about three months at the missionaries' printing office. 'They have so little. All they eat is cold rice and broth. And they sleep on a wooden plank with just a blanket over them.'

One day Imamiya rode in the passenger seat of his father's tiny delivery truck and visited the printing plant. Father and an apprentice were delivering a shipment of paper from the paper wholesaler at Sakura-chō. While his father and the apprentice did their work, Imamiya kicked around pebbles at the entrance to the Western-style house, which had become like a haunted house through exposure to the winds and rain. From time to time he heard the blast of steam whistles from the harbour. Just then, Imamiya noticed a single priest climbing from the bottom of the hill, using an umbrella in place of a walking-stick. The missionary, his head closely cropped, looked exhausted. He was frighteningly skinny. He seemed to be at pains to climb the hill, and half-way up he stopped, removed his sweat-clouded glasses and wiped them with a handkerchief while he got his breath back. Then he put his glasses on again and continued up the hill.

When the missionary saw Imamiya, an almost tearful smile ignited behind his round glasses, and in a faint voice he said: 'Konichiwa'. When Imamiya retreated two or three steps and hid behind the truck, the missionary disappeared in the direction of the printing shop.

For a long while Imamiya remembered the weary figure of that missionary, the sad smile that had flashed from behind his round glasses, and the hollow-cheeked face. He remembered the image, but he had no other impressions and virtually no other recollections of the foreigners. Thereafter the printing shop vanished and the foreign missionaries moved from Ōura to Sotomachi in the heart of the city.

The tour coach, loaded with the Japanese who had finished their lunch and shopping, set out once again. When they returned to the hotel near Saski Park, their time was free until dinner, but most of them, weary perhaps from their lack of sleep the previous night, kept to themselves in their rooms.

Following Tamura's lead, Imamiya lay down on his hard bed and tossed around until evening. Watching the snoring Tamura, who had wrapped a camel-coloured stomach-warmer round his abdomen, Imamiya thought of the name Kolbe, and wondered if by chance one of the missionaries he had encountered in the past had been Kolbe. A pain like a pinprick jabbed at the core of his heart. The figure of the languorous priest, with his round glasses and his smile, loomed before him, and the expression on the man's face stung Imamiya's heart. He got out of bed and shook his head to exorcize that expression. Tamura was still sleeping soundly. When Imamiya pressed his face against the window, the lights in Saski Park shone a pale white, and he could see hunched-over men wearing fur hats returning home from work through the lingering snow.

That night, Imamiya bought a woman.

After dinner, Shimizu escorted his Japanese clients to a night-club in Defilad Plaza. The show had already got under way, and an orange light in the middle of the crowded hall illuminated the tricks being performed by the entertainers.

Once they were seated, the Japanese men followed Shimizu's instructions and turned to look behind them, and their eyes all darted across the women who leaned against the back wall smoking cigarettes. Pretending to watch the show, the women were catching the eyes of the patrons. Imamiya's eyes met those of a woman who must have been about the same age as his eldest daughter, but she walked off towards the foreigners' seats. When he headed for the rest-room, he passed by the small, chestnut-haired woman. After he had washed his hands and came out again, she was standing in the same spot, staring up at him. Their transaction was concluded then and there.

'Did you find any good women?' Tamura brought his lips to Imamiya's ear. 'I got one who speaks Japanese. When I spoke to her, she winked and started saying: "Kombanwa, konichiwa, Mitsubishi, Sony." It's that woman over there. You can have her if you want.'

Imamiya answered that he had already found a partner, and half-way through the show he got up. Shimizu beckoned to him, handed him a piece of paper with the name of their hotel written on it, and told him to show it to the taxi-driver when he wanted to return.

The small woman was waiting for him at the exit of the night-club. She wore an overcoat with white fur round the collar, a fur hat and boots. When she saw Imamiya she smiled and went to fetch his coat from the cloakroom. Then she slipped her arm through Imamiya's and held on to him so that he would not slip on the icy snow outside the door. She began speaking to him in English, but since Imamiya could not understand her, he answered 'Hai, hai' in Japanese. She opened the door of a tiny car and had him get into the passenger seat. She started up the engine, but the car showed no signs of moving. When it finally surged forward, Imamiya said 'Ok', and she smiled and responded, 'Ok!'

They drove endlessly along the road, which was almost void of cars or people. Unlike Tokyo, on a winter's night the roads of Warsaw were deserted. Cold and shivering like an indigent, Imamiya felt the need to urinate again. From time to time the woman would speak to him in English, but he merely answered 'Hai, hai'.

Her apartment was in a five-storey building. They avoided the lift and climbed up the stairs that still smelled of cement. Their loud footsteps echoed in the empty apartment building. The woman opened the door and switched on the light. A refrigerator peered whitely from the eight-mat room, and he saw two chairs and a poster of some male actor hanging on the wall. When he came out of her bathroom, she had made him a whisky on the rocks. The bed was concealed behind a thick curtain. While he took a couple of gulps of his drink, she went to run some hot water in the bathroom. Imamiya stood up and went to the window to look outside, but all he could see was a building that appeared to be a warehouse.

Two or three books written in Polish stood on a tiny desk, and several photographs and religious pictures had been pasted on the wall directly behind the desk. One of the photos seemed to be of her family, and depicted a working-class husband and wife and a young girl. To the side was a picture of the Madonna, and mixed in with several Christmas cards was a reproduction of a portrait of a man drawn in black ink. The man was looking directly out at Imamiya, with a closely shaved head, round glasses and sunken cheeks. Imamiya remembered that weary expression. It was the foreigner who had painfully climbed the hill at Ōura that day in summer. It was the missionary who had stopped midway up the hill to wipe his clouded glasses, and had greeted Imamiya with a 'Konichiwa'.

When the woman came out of the bathroom in a dressing-gown, she spoke to Imamiya, who was staring intently at the portrait.

'That's Kolbe.'

The Box

I have placed several pots of *bonsai* trees and plants in my Harajuku office, so that they can provide a little warmth to my heart when I take a break from work. I call them *bonsai*, but they're really nothing so grand. I've just lined up a few cheap potted plants that I have bought every year at the plant market as I've strolled of an evening beside Shinobazu Pond at Ueno, in search of some relief from the stifling heat of summer.

When I sleep over in my office, the first thing I always do, after waking up in the morning and washing my face, is feed some seed and greens to the tiny birds I keep. Then it's my habit to give the plants some water. But last summer, a female editor who had come to my office on business, told me: 'Did you know that when you're watering your plants, if you talk to them they can understand you? You probably think that's nonsense, but give it a try.' A gentle-hearted, married woman brought up in the downtown *shitamachi* district of Tokyo, she is very fond of plants.

To be frank, I was sceptical about her remarks. I thought it was ridiculous, but at the same time I felt there was a chance that plants had some kind of special faculty, so that even if they could not understand human speech, they might be sensitive to the wishes we expressed for them.

At the time, I had just planted some morning-glory seeds in a pot. I've been fond of morning glories since my childhood, and I wanted to be able to see their large blossoms each morning in the corner of my stifling office.

At the beginning of the day after the editor suggested it to me, each time I watered the morning glories I said to them: 'Please have lots of flowers.' But I realized how insinuating and self-seeking my voice must have seemed to the flowers, so the next time I took a deep breath and spoke to them in all earnest.

My one-sided entreaties continued day after day. As if my petitions had been granted, that summer the single pot of morning glories produced a mass of coiling buds which started turning the colour of strawberry ices, and two or three days later when I opened my eyes in the morning, I was greeted by beaming flowers.

If that had been the end of it, I should have thought nothing out of the ordinary had occurred. But when summer drew to a close, I began to speak differently to the morning glories.

'Don't wither up on me. Keep on blooming.' With these words of encouragement, I poured water on them.

As a result, to my surprise the morning glories kept producing flowers into the autumn. Of course it wasn't one or two a day like it had been in the summer, but at least two blossoms a week delighted my eyes.

'Take a look at this morning glory,' I boasted to the housekeeper. 'It seems to understand human speech.'

'It's true,' she responded. 'This is the first time I've seen morning glories blooming in November.'

'All right, then, since this really works, I'm going to make them bloom during the winter too!'

I doubt anyone will believe what I'm going to say next, but I have a photograph of myself holding a pot with large blooming flowers while snow is falling outside. It's quite true. The photograph that proves it all, a noteworthy photograph that ought to be published in the *Guinness Book of Records*, is pasted in my photo album.

It was the day after a heavy snow had fallen in Tokyo. Despite the weather outside, in my office the large, red morning glories seemed to be spreading their arms proudly. I asked my housekeeper to take a photograph, and I went and stood outside my apartment building with the pot in my arms.

Passers-by stared at me wide-eyed. I said nothing, but I was filled with pride.

Exactly what is it I want to say, starting with such an anecdote?

What I'm trying to express is the fact that humans and animals are not the only ones who have hearts and language and faculties. Things we tend to think of as simple objects – even stones or sticks – have some kind of power living inside them. That's what I'm trying to say.

This happened ten years ago.

Towards the end of summer, I was puttering through a village in Shinshū in a car. In a small cottage in a place called Naka Karuizawa I had been working on a rather long novel, and in late summer, as all the summer villa owners were finally taking their leave, I had somehow finished off the novel, and had decided that I wanted to travel the old highways through Komoro and Ueda and Saku that still retained the smells of the Shinano region.

I had been to Komoro and Ueda many times over, and when I stopped the car I took on the look of a man who knows his way around, peering into old temples and sliding open the soiled glass door of an antique shop I stumbled across.

In a hushed afternoon back-street in Ueda, I found a tottering antique shop that also dealt in used furniture. When I opened the badly hung door, to the left stood a bureau-shaped medicine cabinet that doctors in the old days had used, while pot-hooks hung down from the ceiling, and at the foot of the stairs rustic-looking saucers and a wash-basin had been piled up. The prices of such items have escalated markedly in Tokyo antique shops recently, but ten years ago out in the countryside they were sold at such cheap prices that no one gave them a second glance.

An old woman was leaning against a rectangular *hibachi*, reading a newspaper.

I picked through several objects, until finally my eyes lighted on one. 'What's this?' It was a commonplace box, nothing more than a wooden box wrapped in brightly coloured paper. But inside was a stack of pamphlets, their inks faded from exposure to the sunlight. There were hymn collections and pamphlets from a Protestant church, and children's stories about Jesus. It even contained an old Bible. When I flipped through the Bible, several picture postcards fell from between its foxed pages. The sentences on the postcards had been written in foreign characters. The reverse sides were decorated with photographs of foreign cities and drawings of Santa Claus. A volume resembling a photo album was buried beneath all these items.

Unrelated to my profession as a writer, I am a man of ardent curiosity. I pulled out the faded album and began leafing through it because the worms of curiosity began squirming inside me. But, for some reason, only three photographs were pasted inside the album. There were obvious signs that seven or eight other photographs had been torn out.

'Excuse me, ma'am,' I called out to the woman by the *hibachi*. 'Is this box for sale?'

'Which box is that?' She slowly got to her feet and walked over near me. 'Oh, that. Well, yes, it's for sale, but there's not much point in buying a lot of rubbish like that.'

'That's true. It can't be called antique, after all.'

'I imagine he must have brought it along with some other things from a foreigner's house in Karuizawa. My husband, you see . . .'

'Your husband?'

'After the war ended, they sold off furniture and wall clocks from the foreigners' villas. He probably brought this along with some of the other things.'

'How much do you want for it?'

The old woman peered at me, then answered pityingly: 'Something like this, yes, you can have it for nothing. It's just junk.'

'I couldn't do that.'

I don't remember how much I ended up giving her. I doubt if I parted with more than around 500 yen. She thanked me over and over again, but her eyes made it clear she regarded me as a fool for buying something like this box.

I paid money for what was obviously rubbish because of the old Bible, and because one of the three photographs pasted in the album depicted the old highway through Karuizawa during the war.

It sounds a bit quaint to talk about 'the old highway', but today it's become the main street of Karuizawa, and come summer both sides of the road are jammed like chocolate boxes with branch outlets of Tokyo shops. Along this road bustling throngs of young people, each looking the same and each dressed in the same styles, scurry back and forth.

But the old Karuizawa highway in that photograph appeared to be a scene from either before or during the war. The vista it presented was dark and forlorn and gloomy, like a film set after shooting has been concluded. I remember that scene, however, because I came to Karuizawa once or twice during the war. For that reason, I did not feel that I had lost anything by buying the wooden box decorated with brightly coloured paper, both as a token of the past and as an object of curiosity.

In the dining-room of my cottage that evening, I positioned a small electric stove next to me (when it rains in Karuizawa, even at the end of summer, it turns quite chilly inside my mountain cottage) and began looking through the photographs on the postcards and the horizontal characters scrawled on them.

Fortunately for me, a number of the postcards were written in English and French, which I could read, while the remainder were in incomprehensible German. From the addresses, I was able to determine that the postcards had been sent to a woman with the French-sounding name of 'Mademoiselle Henriette Lougert'. Though the name sounds French, one cannot say with any certainty that this woman was French herself. There could be Belgians with such a name, and it is possible that a woman from Canada could have the name as well. In any case, convincing myself on my own authority that the statute of limitations had already passed, I haltingly began to read the words on the postcards.

They all seemed to have been written by her friends and acquaintances, and the contents asked for news about or inquired after the health of her father, who was also living in Japan; a husband and wife wrote that they were in Madrid, but that an infant delivered by their friend, Madame Blange, had died; another complained that life in Rome had grown exceedingly difficult. One declared that its author was absorbed in reading Tolstoy and Turgenev, and described what the children were doing. There was even a postcard that asked, half-jokingly, whether Japan was really like the country that appears in *Madame Butterfly*.

Sliding my feet closer to the electric heater, then pulling them away again, I wondered what kind of woman this Henriette Lougert had been. It occurred to me that she might have been the wife of a Protestant minister. I had heard before that a number of missionaries from Canada had come to Karuizawa in the old days to escape the summer heat. I even had the impression that there had been a teacher of that name at the Athénée Français at Ochanomizu, which I had attended five or six times and then left many years ago.

In addition to the photograph of the old highway, the album contained a picture of some foreign women carrying parasols as they picked flowers – there were two or three Japanese children with them – and a photograph of the railway station on the Kusakaru line that had once stood below the old highway. Each picture was yellowed and faded, and filled me only with a sense of the passage of time. I imagined that the foreigners and Japanese who appeared in these photographs were all dead by now. Such depressing thoughts must be the result of my advanced age.

Several days later, I removed the photographs from the album and strolled down the old highway, which was still alive with festive activity even though the end of summer was at hand. From time to time I pulled out a dim photograph and compared it with my surroundings, alternatingly experiencing surprise then delight at how much the same scene had changed over the years.

Now I remember. As you climbed the old highway, there had once been an old hotel, the Tsuruya, which was frequented by such writers as Hori Tatsuo, and on a back-street nearby had stood a laundry. I remembered that the owner of the laundry was a man who knew all there was to know about wartime Karuizawa. *I ought to ask that old man*.

I passed by any number of shops that were plastered with signs reading BARGAIN or DISCOUNT, jostling again and again against crowds of young people dressed in tennis outfits and slurping soft ice-cream, until I finally reached the cleaners called Tsuchiya. Regrettably, the owner was out on business. I showed his wife the photographs and asked if she knew any of the people in them.

She shook her head. 'My family's from Iwamurata. I don't know anything about what this place was like during the war. When my husband gets back, I'll get him to phone you.'

I left the photographs with her, and by the time I got back to my cottage in Naka Karuizawa, the phone was already ringing.

'I'm sorry. I was out on some business.'

'I told your wife what this is all about. Do you happen to know the foreigners in the pictures?'

'It's Mademoiselle Louge. I knew her.'

The laundryman called Mademoiselle Lougert 'Mademoiselle Louge', which I suppose is what the locals in Karuizawa must have called her.

'She lived up by Mt Atago . . . the villa is still there. A Japanese bought it after the war, though.'

Mt Atago stands at the rear of the old highway. A friend lived there one summer, but he complained that the humidity was tremendous. But because it's Karuizawa, summer homes have been built up there for many years.

'But sir, how did you end up with a photo of Mademoiselle Louge?'

'I just ran across it in an antique shop in Ueda.'

'In Ueda, eh?' For some reason, the laundryman went silent for a moment. I sensed that there was something to his silence. Call it a writer's intuition, which is unusually accurate. The story which follows is a summary of what the laundryman hesitantly told me the following day, after I brought him a bottle of whisky and we sat down to drink it.

A dark, gloomy, at times even dismal atmosphere hung over Karuizawa during the war, an atmosphere that young people today could not begin to imagine. The atmosphere resulted from the fact that foreigners from various nations, on the pretext that they were being evacuated from military targets, were assembled here, and while on the surface they led normal lives, in reality they were under surveillance by the Japanese secret police and the military police.

Also, in the beginning, they were provided with special rations that were better than the food the Japanese were eating, but eventually, once everything grew scarce, they could not even lay their hands on black-market rice or potatoes, since they had no connections in the provinces, and they began to suffer from malnutrition. They started to roam about the villages near Karuizawa, begging people to sell them eggs or milk.

Mademoiselle Louge (though 'Lougert' is the correct pronunciation) was the daughter of a minister who had come to Japan to proselytize, and each summer for years they had come to Karuizawa to escape the heat. When Mademoiselle Louge was nineteen, her Japanese mother died of tuberculosis, and thereafter she worked as a typist at an embassy in Tokyo while she looked after her ageing father. When the war turned fierce, the Japanese government advised all foreigners to return to their homelands, but her father, who was a citizen of a neutral nation, applied for and received permission to live in Japan because of his illness.

When bombing raids on Tokyo became an almost daily occurrence, the embassy where Mademoiselle Louge worked took refuge in Karuizawa. She took her infirm, elderly father and moved into their mountain cottage near Mt Atago.

Having come here every summer since her childhood, she knew the people of the town well. As a result, she was able to obtain food initially without much difficulty.

Once the villagers began to run short of foodstuffs themselves, however, they stopped sharing rice and potatoes with Mademoiseile Louge and her father. Crop yields were anything but abundant in this tranquil, impoverished region.

It was not unusual in those days to see foreigners set out on bicycles, knapsacks hanging from their backs, to try to buy food as far away as Furuyado and Oiwake. Mademoiselle Louge was one of their number. But neither the peasants of Furuyado nor of Oiwake had sufficient rice or wheat to share with outsiders.

When bombs began to fall on Tokyo, some people burned out of their homes fled on foot to the Karuizawa area. These people begged food from the farmhouses they passed along the way, but once that became an everyday occurrence, the villagers began refusing, and one night in the ice-house, the cellar where ice cut in the winter was stored, a man was found dead with straw crammed into his mouth.

In these circumstances, the foreigners too shed all their pride and pleaded like beggars for food, but the villagers could only shake their heads.

It was during such times that Mademoiselle Louge met a young Japanese man. In a settlement at some remove from Karuizawa she wandered from house to house seeking milk and potatoes for her father, and at each house she was refused. Just then, a young man on a bicycle happened along. The artless young man had close-cropped hair and wore work clothes, and when he heard Mademoiselle Louge's story, he went to talk to the master of the farmhouse from which she had just been turned away. When he returned, the young man reported: 'He's says they'll give you just a little.'

What he sold her, however, could hardly be called ' a little', for she left with her knapsack stuffed with potatoes. Moreover, the young man generously strapped the knapsack on to his bicycle-rack and went with her as far as the railway station.

'Every once in a while, I can bring you over some potatoes. Please give me your address,' the young man said curtly as the whistle of a train sounded far off in the mountains. 'I sometimes have work in Karuizawa.'

He said he worked in the district post office. When Mademoiselle Louge asked why he had not been enlisted in the army, he told her he had been drafted but was sent home the very same day because of pleurisy. Then he divulged that his health had improved and he was waiting to be inducted a second time.

These were times when it was dangerous to rely upon the kindness and the words of others, but Mademoiselle Louge had the distinct feeling that this young man actually would come to Karuizawa with food for her. There had been that much of the country boy's earnestness in his face.

When two weeks, then three weeks passed with no sign of him, however, Mademoiselle Louge abandoned hope.

It was late that autumn when the young man turned up, on a cold day of gloomy, incessant rain. He brought the promised potatoes, as well as apples and a bottle of goat's milk. When Mademoiselle Louge returned from the embassy, her father was sitting in his rocking-chair and, to her surprise, sitting beside him was the young man, snapping dried twigs and stoking the fire in the stove. Because her feeble father could not do any physical work, the young man had asked if there were any chores he could do until Mademoiselle Louge came home from work, and so he had been cutting firewood and chopping logs with an axe.

He joined them for an evening meal of steamed potatoes. The Louges had nothing else to offer him but some jasmine tea from Hong Kong.

After the young man had gone home in the rain, her father smiled and said: 'That Japanese fellow is a good boy.'

'He really is,' Mademoiselle Louge replied.

Thereafter, as though his first visit had been the turning-point, the young man came often. And he always brought something in secret. Once he even brought a can of marinated beef that was impossible to obtain.

'This stuff is hard to come by,' he said responding to her look of amazement. 'A relative gave it to me.' He would add nothing to that clipped explanation. How kind he is, Mademoiselle

Louge thought. In gratitude she wrapped a book in paper and gave it to him, saying: 'Here is some nourishment for your heart. You have given my father and me nourishment for our bodies. In return, I give you nourishment for your heart.'

The heart nourishment was a Bible. Mademoiselle Louge's father was a minister, and she shared the same faith, so she hoped more than anything that this pure young man could also come to know the teachings of God.

The young man accepted the book and thumbed through it. 'I'll try reading it,' he said, putting it into the bag that hung from his shoulder.

She was gripped by a desire, like that of an elder sister or a mother's love, to apply even more polish to this simple, honest young man's character.

'Umm . . . we have to do this very quietly, since the police are troublesome, but on Christmas Eve my father and I and some friends are getting together at the church on the old highway. We'll be offering prayers there. Would you like to come, Mr Fujikawa?'

Fujikawa was the young man's name. His face stiffened for a moment when she asked the question, but he answered: 'At night?'

'Ah, I suppose it's too far to come from your village.'

'Well . . . could I bring a friend?'

'Of course you can. Is it a female friend?'

'No,' he blushed. 'A man.'

Mademoiselle Louge was confident in her heart that a friend of Fujikawa's could be trusted.

On Christmas Eve, some fourteen or fifteen of the foreigners who had been evacuated to Karuizawa assembled at the church. There was no sign of Fujikawa or his friend, so around 8 p.m. they began their prayers, and from his chair Mademoiselle Louge's father related the story of the birth of Jesus.

Midway through the story, Mademoiselle Louge noticed Fujikawa and a rustic-looking, middle-aged man peering at them through the window of the church.

She was thrilled, convinced that God had given them a

wonderful Christmas present. Beaming, she brought the two men into the church, and once her father's recitation was concluded, she introduced them to her friends. The middle-aged man bowed his head deeply to the foreigners, and seemed in all respects to be filled with gratitude. Prayers were resumed, and after the Christmas observance the group chatted together until nearly midnight over home-made bread and the choicest black tea they had been able to find. Mademoiselle Louge and some other foreigners who could speak Japanese interpreted for the two men, and they seemed to have quite an enjoyable time. When they stole quietly outside, the chill of the night air was extreme, but the stars glimmered brightly and all befitted the image of the holy night.

The next day, as Mademoiselle Louge was about to set out for the embassy-in-exile where she worked as a typist, a man she had never seen before was waiting for her in the roadway.

'You are Miss Louge?'

'Yes.'

'I'm from the military police. We'd like to talk to you, so please come with me.'

The tone of his voice made it clear she had no choice. As she stood there in astonishment and fear, he stepped up beside her and led her down the frozen road in the direction of the old highway.

The office of the military police in those days stood right next to the Karuizawa railway station, and sometimes they would interrogate suspicious-looking visitors as soon as they stepped off the train. Mademoiselle Louge was not taken to that office, but instead to a villa surrounded by a spacious yard and set apart from the neighbouring houses.

She was placed in a room with no furnishings other than an unlit stove, a crude table and two chairs. There was no decoration of any kind, and the bare walls were covered with stains. Outside the window she could see the wintry forest, its trees stripped of their leaves. Finally she heard footsteps and the door opened, and in came the middle-aged man, Ono, who had accompanied Fujikawa to the church the previous night. His timid, obsequious behaviour from the night before had vanished, and he seated himself in one of the chairs, spreading his legs arrogantly. Fujikawa stood behind him.

'In terms of nationality,' Ono said with a smile, 'you are a foreigner, but your mother was Japanese. Do you consider yourself a Japanese while you're here, or a foreigner?' Once he had extracted from a cowering Mademoiselle Louge an oath that she had not forgotten her identity as a Japanese, he suddenly spoke to her gently: 'Well, then, do you think we could get you to do something for Japan?'

Throughout the interrogation, Fujikawa stood at the back, his honest-looking face tightly constricted.

The help they wanted was for Mademoiselle Louge to inform them of the sources of telephone calls and mail coming into the embassy where she was employed.

'What do you think? Does that sound distasteful to you?' Ono mumbled as he drummed on the table with his index finger. In the forest outside the window, a wild bird shrieked.

Though Mademoiselle Louge could have known nothing about it, a secret peace initiative was being advanced under the leadership of statesmen from a faction opposed to Prime Minister Tōjō Hideki who had left Tokyo and come to Karuizawa to escape the air raids. A plan had been advanced among their ranks to request that the neutral nation which had hired Mademoiselle Louge serve as intermediary for their peace proposal. The secret police were naturally keeping a close eye on the group's movements.

Fearfully, Mademoiselle Louge shook her head. Her beliefs would not sanction such a contemptible act.

'So, you don't like the idea? That creates some difficulties.' Ono stretched his words out slowly. 'Then shall I turn you over to Fujikawa?' He rose from his chair. 'Don't feel you must hold back because she's a woman.' With that, he disappeared.

'Take my advice. Please co-operate with us.' Fujikawa spoke pleadingly. 'If you don't, I'll have to hurt you. Your father may also be harmed. What we're asking you is very important for Japan's war effort.'

Mademoiselle Louge began to shake when she thought of her old, frail father being tortured.

'Please don't do this. I beg you.'

'It can't be helped. I don't want to do this myself, but orders are orders.'

'I . . . I can't do it. I'm too frightened.'

'Don't worry about it. All you have to do is make sure they don't discover you.'

At that moment, Ono came back into the room.

'What's the verdict, Fujikawa? Has she agreed?'

'No, but I think she will soon.'

Ono seized Mademoiselle Louge's hair and slammed her head into the table.

'Your boss was at that gathering last night, wasn't he?' He ground her face into the table with even greater force. 'You're not dealing with children here!'

'What if we gave her a day to think it over?' Fujikawa tossed her a lifeline from the side. It was their technique to trade off between a whip and a lollipop.

She was released for that day. But the following day a man was waiting for her on the frozen road. Thinking of her elderly father, she had no other choice. She agreed to co-operate.

Fortunately for Mademoiselle Louge, none of the kind of phone calls the police were expecting came in to the embassy, and not a single letter from a Japanese that could be construed to touch on the peace initiative arrived in the mail. At first Ono suspected that she was hiding information, but when Fujikawa dressed up as a plumber hired to repair some frozen sewer pipes and searched the embassy, he could find no signs of a conspiracy either.

Most likely, the people involved in the peace initiative had guessed what the military police were up to and had been careful not to blunder.

At the end of his story, I asked the laundryman how he had learned of these events.

'Well, you see, I had a cousin who was in the police then. He told me about it after the war.'

The story was not all that surprising to me. In gathering material for stories, I had heard even more frightening accounts of the activities of the military police in Karuizawa. I have written about such events elsewhere, and even used them in altered form in my play, *The Rose Palace*.

But the laundryman's story was not finished.

'About a year after the war ended, Mademoiselle Louge's father died, but she didn't go back to Tokyo. She stayed in Atago. She continued with her typing, and taught foreign languages to the young ladies, and she worked for the church as well.'

Then one day an American jeep carrying MPs came from Nagano in search of Mademoiselle Louge. This was perhaps six months after her father's death. At the time, Tokyo and virtually every other part of Japan had been reduced to scorched earth, and the people were about to face their second autumn of starvation and cold. Concurrently, individuals who had co-operated in the military effort and committed war crimes were being interrogated and put on trial, one after another. She was placed in the jeep and taken to Nagano city. There she was questioned by a US military interrogator about her activities during the war. She was asked whether she had been subjected to torture by the military police.

Mademoiselle Louge shook her head. The lieutenant who was examining her looked at her peculiarly and asked: 'Are you sure?'

'I am sure,' she answered.

'Then you don't know these men?' He had an MP open the door. From the shadows of the doorway stepped Fujikawa and Ono, their faces gaunt, dressed in US Army fatigues. 'Are you sure these men did nothing to you?'

At that moment, Mademoiselle Louge recalled with stark clarity how, on that winter morning, these men had clutched at her hair, rammed her head into the table, and threatened and intimidated her. An unspeakable anger swept through her breast.

'They did nothing to you?'

'I remember these men,' Mademoiselle Louge answered. 'These men . . . I. . . .' She paused. 'They gave me and my father potatoes. They brought us goat's milk. We were starving then.'

An interpreter translated precisely Mademoiselle Louge's reply for Fujikawa and Ono. With lowered eyes they listened to the unexpected words.

'I heard that, much later on, one of the two men went and visited Mademoiselle Louge in a Tokyo hospital. I suppose he must have gone to say thank you. She had contracted cancer and didn't have much time left. I feel sorry about that.'

At the height of the war, I had stayed for a couple of weeks in a hamlet called Furuyado near Naka Karuizawa. I was a college student, and I remember one foreign woman who came to the farmhouse where I was staying and asked in broken Japanese if she could buy some eggs. Mademoiselle Louge had been one of those foreign women evacuated to Karuizawa.

I left the laundry and headed for the bus-stop, walking along an alleyway behind the old highway. Young men and women were riding around the back-street on rented bicycles and taking photographs of one another.

I returned to my cottage and had another look through the materials in the box. As I glanced absent-mindedly at the postcards addressed to Mademoiselle Louge – actually, to Mademoiselle Lougert – I suddenly noticed something strange. Various names were written in as senders of the postcards, but their addresses were peculiar. One was from a certain number in Luke Avenue in Rome. Another was from an address in Matthew Street in Madrid. Luke and Matthew are, of course, names of two of the four Gospels in the Bible. In fact, all of the addresses on the postcards had the names of one of the Gospels.

I stared at them for some time. Then, struck by a thought, I pulled out the old Bible from the wooden box. It was musty, and its pages had turned brown from the humidity.

With a postcard return address of '10–5 Viale S. Luca, Rome', I turned to the fifth verse of the tenth chapter of Luke. There it was written: 'And into whatsoever house ye enter, first say, Peace be to this house.' The message on the card said: 'The baby at Madame Blange's house has died of diphtheria. It is very sad. But Madame has recovered emotionally.'

I caught my breath. This may be just arbitrary speculation on my part, but I began to wonder if this was not an allusion to the fact that peace negotiations had broken down.

The next postcard was addressed from '27–1 Calle S. Mateo, Madrid' and contained the message: 'Recently I've been reading Tolstoy and Turgenev.' I knew without even opening the Bible that the first verse of the twenty-seventh chapter of Matthew's gospel described the convening of a meeting by the Sadducees to discuss whether Jesus ought to be killed. Tolstoy and Turgenev were, of course, Russian authors. Linking these two ideas, I thought of the Yalta Summit where the United States, Great Britain and the Soviet Union met to discuss the conclusion of the war.

There was, of course, no proof for any of this. It could be nothing more than my imagination. But wasn't it possible that friends of Mademoiselle Louge who had already returned to their homelands were conveying news of the war situation as they understood it to Mademoiselle Louge and her father in this fashion? And . . . and perhaps she had placed these postcards in her Bible, which she would leave on the prayer altar of the church. Someone would open it up, and pass the news to someone else.

I grew excited. But it was an unfounded excitement, perhaps nothing more than a phantom. And yet, had Mademoiselle Louge hoped that, after her death, this Bible and these postcards would pass into the hands of someone like me? I couldn't help but feel that, in fact, these several postcards, filled with the truth of the matter, had taken on a will of their own, and had been waiting patiently inside the wooden box for many years until they could be read by someone like me.

Perhaps I think up such nonsensical, irrational things because I am getting old. That's why I speak to every one of the potted plants in my office each morning. I think plants must converse with each other, and I have the impression that trees and rocks and even postcards saturated with the thoughts of men must all speak to one another in hushed voices.

The Case of Isobe

Yaki imo-o. Yaki imo. Piping hot yaki imo-o.

Whenever Isobe reflected back on the moment when the doctor informed him that his wife had incurable cancer, the voice of a street vendor peddling roasted sweet potatoes below the window of the examination-room came back to his ears like a sneering mockery of his dismay.

A man's dull, happy-go-lucky crooning voice.

Yaki imo-o-o. Yaki imo. Piping hot yaki imo-o-o.

'This is the cancer right here. It has metastasized over here as well.' The doctor's finger crawled slowly across the X-ray, almost in rhythm to the potato vendor's voice. 'Surgery will be difficult, I'm afraid,' he explained in a monotone voice. 'We'll try chemotherapy and radiation, but...'

Isobe swallowed hard and asked, 'How much longer will she live?'

'Maybe three months.' The doctor averted his eyes. 'Four at best.'

'Will she be in much pain?'

'We can alleviate a certain amount of the physical pain with morphine.'

The two men were silent for a few moments. Then Isobe asked, 'Would it be all right to use the Maruyama vaccine and some other herbal medicines?'

'Of course. Go ahead and use any folk remedies you want.'

The doctor's uncomplicated approval suggested that there was no longer anything he could do for Isobe's wife.

Once again they lapsed into silence. Unable to bear it, Isobe rose to his feet, and the doctor shifted back towards the X-ray, but the sickening creak of his revolving chair sounded to Isobe like a declaration of his wife's impending death.

I must be . . . dreaming.

It still seemed unreal to him as he walked to the elevator. The idea that his wife might actually die had never entered his thoughts. He felt as though he were watching a movie when suddenly a completely different film was projected on to the screen.

He peered vacantly at the sky, a gloomy colour that winter's evening. He could still hear the voice of the potato vendor outside. *Piping hot yaki imo.* He scanned his brain for the most convincing lie to tell his wife. She would surely see through the workings of his mind with the keen sensitivity of the afflicted. He sat in a chair beside the elevator doors. Two nurses walked past, chatting cheerfully together. Though they worked in a hospital, they were filled with a vigour and a youthfulness foreign to illness and sorrow.

He inhaled deeply and gripped the doorknob of her room tightly. She was sleeping with one arm resting across her chest.

He sat down on the single stool and mulled over the lie he was cooking up in his head. His wife languidly opened her eyes and, seeing her husband, smiled feebly.

'Did you talk to the doctor?'

'Um-hm.'

'What . . . did he say?'

'You're going to have to stay in the hospital for three or four months. But he said you'd be a lot better after four months. So you've just got to tough it out a bit longer.'

Aware of the clumsiness of his lie, he felt a faint layer of perspiration beading on his forehead.

'Then I'll be making your life difficult for another four months.'

'Don't talk nonsense. You're no trouble at all.'

She smiled; he had never spoken so gently to her before. It was a smile all her own. When they were first married and Isobe came home from work exhausted from all the intricacies of human associations, she had been there as he opened the door to welcome him with this enfolding sort of smile.

'When you leave the hospital and have a chance to rest up and get much better...' – Isobe compounded his lie to cover the guilt he felt for his lifelong neglect of this woman – '... we'll go to a hot springs resort.'

'You needn't spend so much money on me.'

'You needn't' – the words reverberated with the same subtle loneliness and sorrow as the voice of the potato vendor far off in the distance. Could it be that she knows everything?

Unexpectedly, as if muttering to herself, she announced, 'I've been looking at that tree for some time now.'

As she gazed through the window of her room, her eyes were directed far away towards a giant ginkgo tree that spread its many branches as though in an embrace.

'How long do you think that tree has been alive?'

'Maybe two hundred years, I'd guess. I imagine it must be the oldest tree around here.'

'The tree spoke. It said that life never ends.'

Even when she had been healthy, his wife had been in the habit every day of speaking like a little girl to each of her pots of flowers as she watered them on the veranda.

'Send me up some beautiful flowers.' 'Thank you for the beautiful flowers.' She had learned to conduct such conversations from her flower-loving mother, and she unashamedly continued the practice even after they were married. But the striking up of a conversation with the ancient ginkgo tree must mean that she had instinctively discerned the shadow veiling her own life.

'So now you're talking to trees?' He laughed at her to shield his own uneasiness. 'Well, why not? We've got some sense now of what's going to happen about your illness, so you can go ahead and have your chats every day with the ginkgo.'

'That's right,' she answered lifelessly. Then, as if sensing her own lack of enthusiasm, she stroked her haggard cheeks with her fingers.

A chime sounded. This signal announced the end of visiting hours. Carrying a paper sack filled with her dirty clothes in his hand, he rose from his chair.

'Well, I suppose I must be going.' He gave a deliberate yawn. Then, extending one hand, he gripped his wife's hand in his. Never once had he done anything so embarrassing before she entered the hospital. Like most Japanese husbands, he was ashamed to present any outward display of his love to his wife. Her wrist had grown decidedly thinner, providing evidence that death was subtly spreading through her body. She responded with her characteristic smile and said, 'You're getting enough to eat, aren't you? Take your laundry over to my mother's.'

'Right.'

He went out into the corridor. He felt as though chunks of lead had been jammed into his chest.

In one corner of the room a television with the volume turned down was broadcasting a vapid game show. Four young married couples were each tossing enormous pairs of dice; if their rolls totalled ten, they would win a three-day, two-night vacation to Hawaii.

Seated beside his sleeping wife, he peered absent-mindedly at the screen. A couple who had rolled a ten joyfully clutched each other's hands. Tiny scraps of confetti floated down from above their heads.

Somewhere in the room Isobe heard someone give a derisive laugh. He had the feeling that 'someone' was purposely parading a happy couple before him on the television just to intensify his agony.

Over many long years, Isobe had often been perplexed and confused by his work and by the interplay of human relations, but the situation in which he had now been placed was in a completely separate realm from that string of daily setbacks. Within three or four months, the wife sleeping before his eyes would most surely be dead. It was an eventuality that a man like Isobe had never considered. His heart felt heavy. He had no faith in any religion, but if there were any gods or buddhas to be contacted, he wanted to cry out to them: 'Why are you bringing this misery upon her? My wife's just an ordinary woman of goodness and gentleness. Please save her. I beg you.'

At the nurses' station Tanaka, the head nurse whose face was familiar to Isobe, was writing something on a chart. She glanced up and nodded towards him, her eyes brimming with compassion.

When he returned to his home in Ogikubo, his wife's mother, who lived nearby, was just putting his dinner into the refrigerator. He reported on his wife's condition, but he left the doctor's diagnosis nebulous. He lost courage when he reflected on the shock his mother-in-law would receive if he told her the truth.

'Dad'll be home early today, so I'd better get back.'

'Thanks for everything.'

'With her in the hospital, this house suddenly seems very large.'

'That's because she's so cheerful by nature.' Inwardly, he repeated his appeal to the gods. *She's plain, but she's a good woman. Please, you must save her.*

When his mother-in-law left, he was struck, just as she had observed, by the emptiness of his house, an emptiness he had not noticed before. It was because his wife wasn't there. Until a month earlier, it had seemed only natural to Isobe that his wife would be at home, and he had neither been particularly conscious of her presence nor even initiated a conversation with her unless there was something he wanted. They had not been able to have children of their own, so they had tried adopting a girl. She had not taken to them, and ultimately they felt as though they had failed. If there was some blame to be placed, it was on the taciturn Isobe, who found it difficult to speak kindly to his wife and daughter and to express his own feelings. His wife was the one who led conversations at the dinner-table, with his responses limited to an occasional 'Uh-huh' or 'That's fine.' Often she would sigh at him and complain, 'Can't you talk to her a little more?'

He began actually talking to his wife after she entered the hospital.

The doctor's prognosis was cruelly precise: less than a month after Isobe was given the news, she developed a fever and began to complain of internal pain. Still she struggled to smile, so as not to cause her husband any anguish, but her hair began to fall out after the radiation treatments, and she moaned faintly, evidently stricken with fierce, lightning-like pain whenever she shifted her body even slightly. Thanks to the chemotherapy, she immediately vomited up anything she ate.

Tormented to see her like this, Isobe entreated the doctor, 'Could you possibly give her morphine?'

'Yes, but if we don't time its use properly, it will simply hasten her demise.'

The doctor had contradicted his earlier comment. The policy at Japanese hospitals, where the goal of practising medicine is to prolong human life, is to draw out the patient's life for every possible day. Although Isobe realized that in the long run his wife could not be saved by such treatment, in his heart lurked the wish for her to live one extra hour, even one extra minute. Yet, when he thought of Keiko gritting her teeth to stop showing her pain, concerned no doubt for the effect her cries would have on her husband, he felt like saying, 'No more! Don't fight it any more.'

One day on his way home from work, when he opened the door to her room for the hundredth time, he was surprised to find her smiling at him.

'You wouldn't believe how relaxed I feel today. They gave me some special IV,' she reported in a spirited voice. 'It's like a miracle. I wonder what kind of medicine it is?'

'Maybe some new antibiotic.' *So they've started the morphine.*

'If this medicine works, I'll be able to leave the hospital sooner. And we can't afford this private room.'

'Don't worry about it. We can handle a month or two of private room bills.'

He had, however, already used up the money she had put into savings so they could take a trip to Spain and Portugal after his retirement. She considered this trip a substitute for the honeymoon they had not been able to take, and she had spread open a map and marked the unseen cities of Lisbon and Coimbra with red circles, which stood out like imprints of happiness. She had even asked Isobe, who had spent nearly two years at his company's American office, to teach her some simple English conversation phrases.

> Not telling the truth
> again today I went out
> of the hospital

> With a shudder, I
> open my eyes and think of
> life without my wife

Recently Isobe had written this wretched doggerel in his appointment book while waiting on a platform bench for his train to arrive. Since he didn't bet on horses or play mah-jong, his only meagre pleasures were drinking *sake*, composing miserable haiku, and playing *go*. He had never shown his poems to his wife. He was the kind of man who was embarrassed to reveal his own feelings openly in words or on his face, the kind of husband who hoped for a relationship in which his wife would understand him even if he did not utter a word.

> So slender it is,
> this outstretched arm of hers with
> its protruding veins

One Saturday evening when he arrived at the hospital earlier than usual after work, he discovered in his wife's room a woman with a broad forehead and large-pupilled eyes wearing a triangular cap on her head.

'She's a volunteer.' Cheerful because the morphine took away her pain, his wife Keiko introduced the woman to her husband. 'This is the first time I've seen a volunteer since I came here.'

'Is that so?' the woman asked as she stared at Isobe. 'The head nurse, Miss Tanaka, asked me to look after your wife. My name is Naruse.'

'Are you ... a housewife?'

'No, I was divorced when I was young. During the week I do something that passes for a real job, but on Saturday afternoons I'm part of the volunteer group here at the hospital.'

Isobe nodded as though interested in her explanation, but inwardly he was troubled. He was afraid that this amateur helper might inadvertently let slip to his wife the true name of her affliction.

'She knows all about how to take care of a patient. She was just helping me eat my supper.'

'Well, we'll put our trust in you.' Isobe bowed his head, putting emphasis on the word 'trust'.

'I'll leave you alone, then, now that your husband's here.'

Naruse Mitsuko nodded her head politely, picked up the tray with half the food still remaining, and left the room. From the way she spoke and the quiet way she closed the door, Isobe decided that she was a volunteer he could rely upon.

'She's good, isn't she?' Keiko sounded as though finding this woman had been her own doing. 'She graduated from the same university as you.'

'Why do you suppose someone like her ... does volunteer work here?'

'Because she's someone like her, silly. She knows all sorts of things.' With a woman's frank curiosity, she mused, 'I wonder why she got divorced?'

'How would I know? You shouldn't nose around in other people's business.' His voice sounded angry; inside, he was worried that the easy familiarity that can develop between women might prompt this volunteer to divulge Keiko's illness to her.

'The strangest thing happened.' Keiko seemed as though she were peering far off into the distance as she spoke to her husband. 'I fell asleep after my IV, and in my dreams I saw the living-room in our house, and I was looking at you from behind. After you'd boiled some water in the kitchen, you started getting ready for bed without turning off the gas to the stove. I yelled as loud as I could to warn you that if you left the teapot there and all the water boiled away, you could start a fire.... But you had this indifferent look on your face. I shouted to you over and over again. But then you turned out the bedroom light....'

Isobe stared fixedly at the opening and closing of his wife's lips as she spoke. Everything she described in her dream had actually happened. The night before, after he turned out the bedroom light and fell asleep, he awoke to an indescribable apprehension in his heart. At that moment, he realized that he had left the gas on in the kitchen, and he sprang to his feet. When he scrambled into the kitchen, the teapot was glowing as red as a cherry.

'Really?'

'Yes. Why?'

Keiko listened with a nervous face as he explained what he had done. Then, with the look of one who has just awakened from a dream, she said, 'Well, perhaps I'm still good for something. They say that dreams can come true, and I suppose sometimes they do.'

Isobe worried that his wife talking to trees and having odd dreams might be an indication of how close death was approaching. When he was a child, his grandmother had told him that people who were about to die could see things that healthy people couldn't.

Her pain was abated with the morphine, but the debilitation of her body was so pronounced that Isobe recognized it even though he came to see her every day. But the morphine left her mind alert.

'Miss Naruse told me something interesting today. She said that scholars have acknowledged that dreams have various profound meanings. What did she say it was called? Oh, dream therapy. She told me that through my dreams I could understand what was in my unconscious mind. But that's all she'd tell me.'

Listening to her story, Isobe for some reason felt uneasy about the large-eyed Miss Naruse. There was something about her that made it seem as though she could see through to the very workings of Keiko's mind.

Once the vitality that the morphine provided suddenly drained away, like the evening glow on a summer's day that flares up for just an instant before darkness takes over, Keiko had to wear an oxygen mask constantly, and her breathing was agitated as she slept. One Saturday evening when he noiselessly opened the door, she lay with her eyes clamped painfully shut, an intravenous needle stabbing into her arm, while beside her the woman volunteer was rubbing her legs. When Keiko heard her husband come in she opened her eyes lethargically, but she no longer flashed her trade-mark smile. In a wispy voice she mumbled, 'I feel like I'm falling ... to the bottom of the earth.' Then she went back to sleep. There was no change in the volunteer's expression as she looked at the patient. He felt as though that icy gaze were saying 'There's no more hope', and an inexpressible pain seized him.

'How has she been today?'

'She was able to talk a little.'

'She doesn't know what's happening.' He lowered his voice to a whisper. 'I haven't said anything to her. I'd appreciate your co-operation.'

'I understand. But ...' Mitsuko said softly, 'your wife may already know. Patients with terminal cancer are far more aware of their approaching death than people around them imagine.'

'She's never said a word to suggest anything like that,' he protested, making sure that his wife was still sound asleep.

Mitsuko's voice continued to run cold as she said, 'That's just out of her consideration for you.'

'You have some cruel things to say, don't you?'

'I'm sorry. But, as a volunteer, I've seen many similar cases.'

'What did my wife talk to you about today?'

'She was worried about how helpless you'd be without her.'

'She was?'

'And she said something peculiar. She said her conscious mind had slipped out of her body and was looking down from the ceiling at the shell of her body lying on the bed.'

'Do you think that's the side-effects of her medicine?'

'It could be. But once in a while patients in the final stages of their cancer have the same experience. None of the doctors or nurses believe them, of course.'

This phenomenon struck Isobe as a portent of his wife's death. Again today the sky was dark grey beyond the window, and he could hear the dull-witted voice of the potato vendor outside the hospital. The pedlar could have no idea what impact his torpid voice had on those who heard it. A scene from Lisbon, with pots of thriving flowers in every window. The shores of the sea at Nazareth, with women in black robes mending their nets on the pure-white beach. If his wife were going to see apparitions, he would rather she saw these kinds of scenes instead of her own corporeal shell stretched out upon the bed.

This incident of the mind fleeing the body was, after all, an omen that the end was near.

The doctor called him over to the nurses' station. 'I think we've got another four or five days. If you're going to send for any relatives . . .'

'Four or five days?'

Behind his glasses, the doctor lowered his eyes. The pocket of his soiled examination coat was crammed with ballpoint pens, thermometers and the like. At times such as this, he had no desire to see the expressions on the faces of his patients' families.

'So soon?' Isobe spoke the meaningless words with lingering hope, though he had not forgotten for a single day that the doctor had initially predicted she would live only three or four months.

'Will she remain conscious until the end?'

'That's hard to say. Very likely she'll go into a coma two or three days beforehand.'

'She won't die in pain, will she?'

'We'll do everything we can to relieve her suffering.'

Finally that day had come pressing in before his eyes. 'Desolation' would not be the proper word to describe his feelings now; it was more the sense of emptiness he imagined he might feel standing all alone on the surface of the moon. Bearing up against that hollow feeling, he quietly gripped the doorknob of her room. Nurse Tanaka and a young assistant were constructing an oxygen tent.

'Ah, your husband's here.' The veteran nurse spoke encouragingly.

'Darling.' With a flutter of her hand she summoned her husband to her bedside, then pointed to the table next to her pillow. 'When it's over . . . look through the diary in here.'

'I will.'

The two nurses knew enough to leave the room, after which Keiko said, 'Thank you for these many years. . . .'

'Don't talk nonsense.' Isobe turned his head away. 'You silly woman, you talk as though you're near death or something.'

'I'm sorry. But I know what's happening. By tomorrow, I may not be able to talk at all.'

There was no more time for shame or embarrassment. Tomorrow the partner he had lived with for thirty-five years could well be leaving this world.

He sat in the chair next to her bed and stared silently at his wife's face. He was weary, but a far deeper exhaustion clouded her face. Sluggishly she opened her eyes a crack and looked at her husband, but it seemed even that caused her pain, and once again she closed them.

Nurse Tanaka came back into the room and placed a new oxygen mask on her face.

'If this bothers you, you can take it off. But this one will be more comfortable for you.'

Keiko did not respond. With her eyes still closed, she continued to breathe, her shoulders heaving.

She slipped into a coma that night. From time to time she would mutter something deliriously. Isobe could do nothing but sit beside her and clutch her hand. Doctors and nurses in endless succession tested her blood pressure, gave her injections, checked her pulse. Isobe contacted her father, mother and younger brother who all lived in Tokyo.

As he hung up the pay-phone and was about to return to her room, a young nurse came running down the hallway towards him. 'Sir, she's calling you. Please hurry.'

When he entered the room, Nurse Tanaka opened the oxygen tent and said in an agitated voice, 'She's trying to say something. Put your ear right up to her mouth.'

'It's me. Me! Do you understand?'

Isobe placed his ear directly by her mouth. In a gasping voice, she was desperately struggling to say something in fits and starts.

'I . . . I know for sure . . . I'll be reborn somewhere in this world. Look for me . . . find me . . . promise . . . promise!'

She spoke the words 'promise . . . promise!' more forcefully than the others, as though these final words were her last desperate plea.

Several days passed as if in a dream. Despite his every effort, he could not convince himself that his wife was actually dead. Over and over again he told himself, *She's gone off on a trip with a friend, she'll be back soon*. Three days later, when the swarm of black automobiles came to a halt in front of the crematorium near the Kōshū highway and the clusters of survivors were swallowed into the building as though on a conveyor belt, and even when they sat waiting their turn for the ceremonies, the same sorts of thoughts filled Isobe's mind. Through the window of the waiting-room he could see the plume of

74

smoke rising from the crematorium's tall chimney, but it reminded him of nothing more than the overcast skies he had often seen from her hospital window. *She's off on a trip*, he mumbled in the general direction of the smoke. *When she gets back from her trip, life will all return to normal.* Disconnected from his thoughts, his lips formed words of appreciation to speak to the assembled mourners.

An attendant came in to announce the beginning of the cremation. Before long, a middle-aged man dressed in a uniform and cap stood in front of Isobe and flipped the switch to the furnace, and a sound like the bullet train rumbling across a steel bridge filled the room. *What is happening? What are they doing?* Even at this point the dumbfounded Isobe had no idea. 'Now if you'll please use these chopsticks to collect the bones and place them in this urn,' the uniformed man declared without expression, sliding out a large black box. Isobe could not bring himself to believe that the strangely pallid fragments of bone strewn in the box were those of his wife. *What the hell is this? What are we doing?* He mumbled to himself as he stood beside his weeping mother-in-law and several other female relatives. *This isn't her.*

The funeral urn was wrapped in a white cloth and, holding it in his arms, Isobe returned to his house with the family members and the Buddhist priest. When he entered the house, the furniture they had sat on together, and the favourite household items she had often used, were arranged just where she had placed them when she was alive. The women in the family began serving plates and bowls of food and glasses of beer to the guests.

'After we hold the seventh-day memorial service,' one relative, the foam from his beer still frothing on his face, observed, 'the next will be the forty-ninth day observance, won't it?' Since this fellow had taken charge of all the arrangements for the funeral, his mind seemed to be full of nothing but the remaining obligations.

'What day next month will the forty-ninth day fall on?'

'It's a Wednesday.'

'I know you're all very busy, so please leave everything to me. We'll handle it with the utmost circumspection.'

'But, Your Reverence,' another man questioned the priest, 'why is it that this gathering is held on the forty-ninth day in Buddhism?'

'Let me explain.' Fingering the rosary beads on his lap, the bald-headed priest had a look of pride as he offered his response. 'In Buddhist teachings, when an individual dies, their spirit goes into a state of limbo. Limbo means that they have not yet been reincarnated, and they wander uneasily about this world of men. Then, after seven days, they slip into the conjoined bodies of a man and a woman and are reborn as a new existence. That is why we have the observance on the seventh day after death.'

'I see.' Hearing this explanation for the first time, the men sat staring at the priest, clutching their glasses of beer.

'So it's every seven days, is it?'

'That's right. And no matter how slow the person is in getting reincarnated, by the forty-ninth day they invariably attain new life by being reborn as someone's child....'

'Hmm.' As one, the group emitted what was either a sigh of curiosity or of relief, but not one of them really believed anything the priest was saying.

'I see. So that's why at Buddhist temples after a funeral they're always talking about the forty-ninth day this, the forty-ninth day that,' one of the group volunteered, but inwardly they all regarded this as a simple money-making measure on the part of the temples.

His wife's delirious ravings echoed in Isobe's ears: 'I know for sure... I'll be reborn somewhere in this world. Look for me... find me....'

As Isobe sat lost in recollection of those words, the gentle priest came up to him, and with a bow of his head said, 'I have finished my duties, so I'll be leaving now.'

When everyone had finally gone, Isobe opened up the two travelling bags he had brought back from the hospital. They contained the items his wife had used while she was there. A dressing-gown, a négligé, underwear, a towel, her toiletries, a clock – and included among all these, the diary she had written in the hospital. It was a small notebook covered in black leather that M. Bank handed out for publicity to all its customers at the year's end. He felt a clutching in his chest as he opened the first page.

Your kimonos and winter clothing: in the paulownia wood box marked A in the closet.

Your spring and autumn kimonos, summer wear, and formal kimonos: in the paulownia box marked B.

Be sure to brush your kimonos and have them cleaned at the end of each season.

Your sweaters and cardigans are in paulownia box C.

I've explained all of this to my mother.

Our savings passbook and personal seal are in a box at the
bank, along with our stock certificates and real estate title papers.
    If you have any questions, talk to the branch manager, Mr
Inoue, at M. Bank, or to our attorney, Mr Sugimoto.

His eyes clouded over, and Isobe hesitated turning the page. On
every page his wife had noted down, one after the other, all the daily
instructions her husband would need in order to avoid problems after
she was dead. *Be sure to turn off the gas before you go to bed; here's how
to clean the bath-tub* – these were all tasks that he had left to his wife
until now. She had explained each of them in simple detail.
    'Do you think I'll be able to do this?' he bellowed towards the me-
morial tablet and photograph of his wife hanging in the living-room.
'You can't just leave the house like this.... Come back... at once!'
    Some twenty days before she died, she had made the following
notation, almost like a memo to herself rather than a journal entry:

22 January
    Cloudy. Another IV today. The veins in my arms have pretty
much collapsed by now, and my arms are covered with blackish
bruises from the haemorrhaging. I've been talking to the ginkgo
tree outside my window.
    'Mr Ginkgo, I'll be dying soon. I envy you. You've been alive
for over two hundred years now.'
    'I wither too, when winter comes. Then in spring, I come back
to life.'
    'But what about people?'
    'People are just like us. Though you die once, you return to life
again.'
    'Return to life? But how?'
    'Eventually you'll understand,' the tree replied.
25 January
    When I think of my clumsy husband, who won't have anyone
to look after him when I'm gone ... I'm filled with concern.
27 January
    In a lot of pain until evening. I can handle the physical pain
with the medication, but my mind ... my mind grows weary from
the fear of death.
30 January
    Miss Naruse came as a volunteer today. She always seems so

serene and so much in control that I end up telling her all the worries and secrets I can't convey to my husband.

'I realize that I'm probably going to die. I haven't said anything to my husband, but . . .'

She had the good grace to smile in response. It was just like her not to offer any empty words of denial or consolation.

'Miss Naruse, do you believe in rebirth?'

'Rebirth?'

'Do you think it's true that, once a person dies, she can be born again into this world?'

She stared straight at me for a moment, but she did not nod her head.

'I can't get rid of the feeling that I'm going to be reborn and meet up with my husband again.'

Miss Naruse turned her eyes towards the window. To the scene I had grown accustomed to seeing day after day after day. The giant ginkgo tree.

'I have no idea,' Miss Naruse muttered. She picked up my dinner-tray and left the room. From behind, she looked hard and cold.

The empty days continued in procession. He stayed late at work, delaying the time of his return home, in an effort to fill the hollow cavity in his heart. He managed somehow to bandage his melancholy by taking his late-working chums at the office out for dinner and drinks. But it pained him to have to return home and look at the items his wife had used. Her slippers, her teacup, her chopsticks, the family budget book, her brief scribblings in the phone book. Every time his eyes rested on these mementoes, a pain like a stab from an awl punctured his chest.

Sometimes he would wake up in the middle of the night. There in the darkness he would try to persuade himself that his wife was sleeping in the next bed.

'Hey. Hey!' he would call out. 'Hey, are you asleep?'

The only response, finally, was black silence, black emptiness, black loneliness.

'When are you coming back from your trip? How long do you plan to desert this house?'

In the darkness he would close his eyes and project images of his wife's face on to the backs of his eyelids. *Where are you, you idiot?*

What are you doing, abandoning your husband like this . . .?

'I know for sure . . . I'll be reborn somewhere in this world. Look for me . . . find me.' Her final ravings continued to ring in the depths of his ears, like a distinct echo.

But Isobe could not bring himself to believe that something so outlandish could happen. Because he lacked any religious conviction, like most Japanese, death to him meant the extinction of everything. The only part of her that was still enduring was the daily items in the house that she had used while she was alive.

When you were still here, Isobe thought, *death seemed so far removed from me. It was as though you stood with both arms outstretched, keeping death from me. But now that you're gone, suddenly it seems right here in front of me.*

The only course left him was to go once every other week to the cemetery at Aoyama, where he would splash water on the Isobe family grave-marker, change the flowers and press his hands together in prayer. This was the only response he could offer to his wife's plea to 'look for me, find me'.

December came. He could not bear spending the holidays in an empty house that was on the brink of disarray, precisely because his late wife had been so fond of the decorations and the special delicacies of the New Year. To his great relief, a niece who was living in Washington DC wrote and invited him to spend his holiday period in the United States. Isobe accepted the invitation, hoping to find some relief from the loneliness that persisted, no matter how busy he kept himself.

He had lived for a time in Washington when he was still single. He drove around the city in his niece's car, but little seemed to have changed. His niece's husband, a researcher at the Georgetown University medical centre, took Isobe to his office on the campus, which reminded him of an old European university, and he walked through the college town, which felt like walking back into the nineteenth century. One evening he found a book on the kitchen counter at his niece's: it was a best-seller written by the famous film star Shirley MacLaine, complete with a photograph of the author on the cover.

'This is Shirley MacLaine, is it?' Isobe asked. 'I really liked her in the early days. I understand she's quite taken with Japan.'

'This is a very popular book right now,' his niece replied.

'What's it about?'

'She writes about her quest for her previous lives.'

'This niece of yours believes in all that nonsense.' Her husband smiled sarcastically. 'Her bookshelf is filled with this kind of stuff – books on New Age science and the like.' With the logic of a doctor, he explained that in America a wave of exaggerated interest in the paranormal and in near-death experiences had recently turned into something of a social craze.

'The good doctor here can only think rationally about everything.' Her cheeks puffed out in displeasure. 'There's all kinds of things in the world you can't explain away with rational argument.'

'That's only because they can't be explained yet. Some day science will decipher them all.'

'But,' Isobe, who had been listening quietly, interjected, 'this book by Shirley MacLaine – well, frankly, I have to admit I don't believe in a previous life or anything – why has it become a best-seller? I'm more interested in the answer to that.'

'There, you see?' Isobe's niece seemed to mistake his curiosity for support of her views. 'I hear that research into these kinds of things has been conducted in all seriousness at American universities ever since the Vietnam War.'

'Only by psychologists who know nothing about science, and some New Age philosophers,' her husband sneered. 'I'm told that there are some people studying this business of previous lives at the University of Virginia.'

'There certainly are. A book by a scholar named Stevenson at the University of Virginia is number three on the best-seller list at our local bookstore.'

'Who's this Stevenson fellow?'

'I haven't read his book yet, but apparently this professor and his staff are collecting data on children from all over the world who claim to have memories of their previous lives, and they're doing a full-scale study of them.'

Sipping the mixed drink she had fixed for him, her husband shrugged his shoulders. This is just too stupid even to talk about, he seemed to be signalling.

Isobe twirled his glass with one hand, once again hearing his wife's final words.

Had she seriously believed in a former life, or in a life to come? A part of her had been naïve enough to carry on conversations with trees and flowers, and to believe in prescient dreams, and Isobe was inclined to think that her rambling comments had been nothing more than the product of an earnest yearning.

But that notion made him realize, with an attendant clutching pain in his chest, how important he had been to his wife throughout her life.

He had not the slightest feelings of endorsement for anything like an afterlife or reincarnation. Like his niece's husband, he had smiled and nodded when she got worked up over her description of the MacLaine book, but he had not meant any of it.

With a yawn, his niece's husband tried to bring the conversation to an end. 'Why do women like to talk about such things?'

'Well, my dead wife also . . .' Isobe started to say, but he stopped himself. Although he did not believe in them, his wife's last words remained a meaningful secret he did not want to reveal to anyone else. They were like a precious memento his wife had bequeathed to him.

While he was killing time in the gift shop at the Washington airport on the day of his departure, he discovered both Shirley MacLaine's *Out on a Limb* and Professor Stevenson's *Children Who Remember Previous Lives* propped in a corner of the display window, labelled as best-sellers. This seemed less like a coincidence than the workings of some invisible power, and though he still did not believe the preposterous things his niece had talked about, he couldn't stifle the feeling that his dead wife had been pushing him from behind, directing him towards the display window. Without even thinking, he bought the books.

He began reading on the plane. A Pan Am stewardess who brought him a drink glanced at the cover of the MacLaine book and said, 'That's a really interesting book. I was fascinated by it.' His niece's claims had been right on target.

Isobe, however, was more impressed with the results of Professor Stevenson's research. The professor reported on a variety of field studies, and there was something trustworthy in the way that he judiciously and objectively noted that 'While these phenomena have unquestionably occurred, we cannot conclude on the basis of these experiences that individuals have had a previous life.' Reading this persuasive study, Isobe began to feel just a glimmer of faith in his wife's last words.

Dear Mr Osamu Isobe

Thank you for your letter of 25 May. I'll try to respond to the questions you raised.

Here at the University of Virginia, we have been conducting studies on life after death under the guidance of Professor Ian Stevenson since 1962. At Professor Stevenson's direction, we have searched out children under the age of three from many nations who claim to have recollections of a previous existence, and we have been collecting testimonials from these children, as well as objective statements from their parents and siblings, and even information regarding their physical characteristics. Our studies form just a part of the research that has been done since the Vietnam War to cast light on near-death or out-of-body experiences, paranormal powers, and other areas of investigation that have borne fruit in the United States.

At the present time, the conditions we place upon instances of 'reincarnation' that have become the objects of our study are as follows:

(1) instances for which a considerable amount of evidence supporting the veracity of the claims exists, which cannot be explained away as clairvoyance, telepathy, or subconscious memory;

(2) instances in which the subject possesses a sophisticated talent (such as speaking a foreign language or playing a musical instrument) which they clearly could not have learned in their present life;

(3) instances in which the subject has markings in the same location as wounds which they received in the previous life they are remembering;

(4) instances in which those experiences labeled as memories display no significant reduction in clarity as the subject ages, and which do not have to be induced through hypnotic trance;

(5) instances in which a large number of the survivors and friends from the subject's past life confirm the person's reincarnation over a long period of time;

(6) instances in which the identification between the subject and the past personality cannot be explained through the influence of parents or other individuals (the reason we put greatest emphasis upon children under the age of three is that at later ages there is an increased possibility that children will confuse and hallucinate random conversations between adults with their own memories).

We insist upon these rigorous conditions because our research has nothing to do with the occult, with obscure religious movements, or with clairvoyants, but is first and foremost an objective, scholarly study.

I should add that in no sense have we concluded at the present time that human beings are in fact 'reincarnated'. We have simply reported the fact that phenomena suggesting the possibility of 'reincarnation' have been isolated in many nations of the world.

We have collected over 1600 cases of 'reincarnation', but, unfortunately, we have only one case in which the subject claimed that her previous life was spent as a Japanese. The details of the case are as follows.

A girl by the name of Ma Tin Aung Myo, who was born in the village of Nathul in Burma in December of 1953, began to talk incessantly about her previous life from the time she was about four years old. One day while she was out walking with her father, she saw an airplane flying overhead and began to wail and shout, displaying evident terror. Thereafter she showed extreme fear whenever she saw an airplane, and when her father questioned her about it, she said it was because she knew she would be shot at. Then she became downcast and began to plead, 'I want to go to Japan.'

With the passage of time she began to reveal that she had been born in the northern part of Japan, that she was married and had children (the number would sometimes vary with the telling), that she was drafted into the army, and while stationed in Nathul, when she was preparing to cook a meal beside a pile of firewood, an enemy plane appeared overhead. She – that is, the Japanese soldier – was standing there in a pair of shorts with a waist-band wrapped around her stomach, when the enemy plane suddenly did a steep dive and began strafing the ground with machine-gun fire. She ran and hid behind the pile of firewood, but a bullet struck her in the groin and she died instantly.

That is the story told by Ma Tin Aung Myo. She later claimed she has the feeling that she ran a small shop in Japan before she was drafted, and that in the army she had cook's duty, and that the Japanese troops were in the process of withdrawing from Burma when she was killed.

Her story does not include the name of the Japanese soldier, or any of the names of his family or the places where he lived. She does, however, dislike Burmese food, and prefers sweet foods and a curry derived from very sugary coconuts. She says over and over that she wants to go back to Japan where her children are, or that she wants to go to Japan when she grows up. Her family reports that Ma Tin Aung Myo mutters to herself in a language they cannot comprehend, but we don't know whether it is Japanese or just some infantile babblings. Strangely enough, she has a scar in the groin area, in exactly the same location where she claims she was shot in her previous life. For more details on this case, I would encourage you to read Professor Stevenson's research report.

I will, of course, be happy to contact you should we come across any more cases in our research in which the subject claims to have been Japanese in a previous existence.

Sincerely,

John Osis

Human Personality Research Division
Department of Psychology
University of Virginia School of Medicine

THE NEW DIRECTIONS *Bibelots*